You Can't Save Them All!

DuMoire

L J Ribar

DuMoire

L J Ribar

Wine Glass PRESS

* * *

First Edition: February 2026

❀ Formatted with Vellum

Chapter 1
The Locked Car

The drizzle started just after midnight, turning the asphalt into a mirror of sodium light and shadow. Kai DuMoire walked with his hands in his jacket pockets, head down, following the familiar route from the late shift at Brennan's Restoration Shop to the studio apartment he rented above a shuttered laundromat. The street was quiet in that particular way summer nights get when the heat finally breaks—windows cracked open, distant television glow, the hiss of tires on wet pavement three blocks over.

The city had a rhythm at this hour. Slow. Muted. Kai preferred it this way.

He'd worked a double shift refinishing a mahogany desk. His shoulders ached. His hands smelled like mineral spirits. His mind was blank in the way it got after repetitive work—empty, drifting.

Almost.

He was halfway down Maple when the pulse hit.

Sharp. Insistent. Threaded with panic. Not sound, exactly—pressure behind his eyes, tightness in his chest that wasn't his own. Kai stopped. His breath caught. The sensation sharpened into something he'd learned to recognize: fear. Animal fear. Close.

He scanned the parked cars lining the curb. Most were dark, empty. Then he saw it—a silver sedan three cars down, driver's side window cracked maybe an inch. Inside, a shape moved. Low to the seat. Panting.

Kai crossed the street.

The dog was a pit mix, brindle coat slick with sweat, pressed against the passenger door. Its eyes caught the streetlight—wide, wet, amber and desperate. The pulse intensified. He felt the animal's thirst like sandpaper in his throat, the heat like weight on his lungs.

He glanced up and down the block. No movement. The house closest to the sedan had its porch light off, curtains drawn.

Kai crouched beside the driver's door and pulled a slim leather case from his jacket. His hands moved automatically—tension wrench, short hook pick. The lock was standard pin tumbler, older model. He slid the wrench into the keyway, applied light pressure, worked the pick in above it. First pin set with a soft click. Then the second. The dog whined—thin, desperate. Kai's jaw tightened. Third pin. Fourth.

The lock turned.

He eased the door open. The smell hit him—overheated fur, urine, stale fear. The dog didn't lunge. It stared, trembling, too exhausted to do more than pant.

Kai reached into his other pocket and pulled out a collapsible water bottle. He filled the cap, held it low. The dog's nose twitched. It leaned forward, tentative, then lapped at the water with a desperation that made something twist in Kai's chest.

He refilled the cap twice more before the dog finally slowed, its breathing evening out. The pulse in Kai's head eased. He set the bottle on the passenger seat, cracked the rear windows another two inches—enough for airflow, not enough to invite theft—then checked the door locks. All manual. Good.

He closed the driver's door, tested the handle. Locked. No scratches on the paint, no sign of entry. The dog watched him through the glass, calmer now, eyes still bright but no longer frantic.

Kai stepped back onto the sidewalk, tucked the pick set into his jacket, and kept walking.

The drizzle thickened into rain. Kai pulled his hood up and turned the corner.

Behind him, across the street from the silver sedan, a second-floor window glowed with the pale light of a smartphone screen. Mrs. Delgado, seventy-three, retired teacher and insomniac, lowered her phone. She'd been filming the whole thing.

But she didn't call the police.

She watched the hooded figure vanish into the rain, replayed the video once, and felt something unfamiliar stir in her chest. Not fear. Not suspicion.

Curiosity.

Kai's apartment smelled like old coffee and sawdust. He dropped his jacket on the back of a chair, kicked off his boots, and went straight to the bathroom sink. His hands were steady. His reflection wasn't. Dark circles under his eyes. Jaw tight.

The memory of the pulse lingered—an echo in his skull, a phantom tightness in his chest. He splashed cold water on his face, gripped the edge of the sink, and counted his breaths. In for four. Hold for four. Out for four.

It helped. A little.

Six months ago, he'd been normal. Or close enough. A locksmith apprentice with decent work ethic and no particular direction. Then came the accident—a T-bone collision at an intersection he crossed every day, a week in the ICU, and a recovery that left him physically intact but fundamentally changed. The doctors called it a miracle.

The first time it happened, he thought he was having a panic attack. Walking past a row of townhouses when the sensation hit— raw, clawing terror that didn't belong to him. He'd followed it to a basement window and found a cat trapped behind a furnace grate, dehydrated and half-starved. He'd broken the lock on the back door, pulled the grate free, and left the cat with a bowl of water and an open exit.

No one saw him. No one knew.

But he knew.

He'd tried explaining it once to his father, Liam. That he could feel things he shouldn't be able to feel. That animals in distress broadcast their fear like a signal he couldn't tune out. Liam had looked at him the way you look at someone who's one bad day away from a breakdown and suggested he talk to someone. A professional.

Kai didn't talk to anyone after that.

The truth was simpler and more complicated. He wasn't hallucinating. The signals were real. He'd tested it enough times to be sure. The problem wasn't whether he could trust his senses. The problem was what to do with them.

Ignore the signals, and the guilt ate him alive. Follow them, and he became something he didn't have a name for. Not a hero. Heroes didn't break into cars at midnight.

He dried his face and dropped onto the futon that served as both couch and bed. The space was small—kitchenette along one wall, a card table with a laptop and a stack of unread mail, a bookshelf crammed with field guides and repair manuals. No TV. No pictures on the walls. Just the basics.

The kind of place you rented when you weren't planning to stay long. Kai had been here eight months. The only personal item visible was a framed photo on the bookshelf—him and Liam, years ago, standing in front of a half-restored sailboat. Both of them smiling.

He didn't look at it much anymore.

He pulled out his phone, checked the time. 12:47 a.m. His next shift at Brennan's started at nine. He should sleep. He wouldn't.

Instead, he opened a notes app and added a new entry.

Maple Street. Silver sedan. Pit mix. Dehydrated, overheated. Owner negligent, not malicious. Left water, increased ventilation. No confrontation.

He stared at the entry, then scrolled up through the list. Fourteen rescues in six months. Cats locked in garages. A rabbit left in a wire cage on a balcony in full sun. A puppy abandoned in a dumpster behind a grocery store. Each one a clean intervention—no damage, no trace, no drama.

He closed the app and set the phone on the floor.

The rain picked up outside, drumming against the window. Kai lay back.

Sleep didn't come. Instead, his mind replayed the rescue in fragments—the dog's eyes in the streetlight, the click of the lock pins, the desperate sound of lapping water.

The pulse came again an hour later—distant this time, muffled. A cat, maybe. Somewhere north. He lay there for ten minutes, jaw clenched, fists tight.

It didn't go away.

It never did.

Kai sat up, pulled his boots back on, and reached for his jacket. He checked his pockets—pick set, water bottle, small flashlight.

The rain was still falling when he stepped outside. The street was empty. He turned north and started walking, following the signal.

The pulse grew stronger with each block. Sharper. More urgent. His pace quickened.

Somewhere ahead, something was waiting. Something afraid.

Behind him, the apartment door swung shut with a soft click.

Inside, on the card table, his phone screen lit up with a notification. A local news blog, auto-posted at 1:15 a.m.

Viral Video: Mystery Hero Rescues Dog from Locked Car

Anonymous footage shows hooded figure breaking into vehicle to save overheated animal. Police investigating. Public reaction: overwhelmingly supportive.

The screen dimmed.

The rain continued.

And somewhere in the city, another animal waited.

Chapter 2
Detective on the Clock

The briefing room smelled like burnt coffee and institutional disinfectant. Detective Sienna Halbrook sat near the back, one elbow on the scarred table, fingers drumming a slow rhythm against her notepad. The overhead fluorescents hummed. Around her, a dozen detectives and patrol supervisors slouched in various states of attention, waiting for Captain Ortiz to finish his opening remarks about budget allocations and overtime restrictions.

Sienna stopped listening after the third mention of "fiscal responsibility." She'd heard this speech before.

She'd transferred to Animal Welfare two years ago, after six years in Homicide left her with insomnia, a failed marriage, and the growing conviction that she was spending her life documenting tragedies instead of preventing them. Animal Welfare was supposed to be different. Smaller stakes. More opportunities for intervention.

It hadn't worked out that way.

She scanned the incident reports Cole had forwarded to her tablet. Seventeen animal-related calls overnight. Three noise complaints about barking dogs. Two reports of strays in traffic—one hit by a car, DOA; the other corralled by a Good Samaritan and dropped at an overcrowded shelter. One dead cat found in a storm drain—natural causes, probably.

And then there was the one that didn't fit: a locked-car incident on Maple Street, resolved before patrol arrived. Owner claimed ignorance. The dog was fine. No charges filed.

Sienna had read enough incident reports to know when something was off. This one had all the markers—too convenient, too clean, too many details that didn't line up.

She tapped the entry, pulled up the attached notes. Responding officer had noted that the car's windows were cracked more than the owner remembered leaving them. No signs of forced entry. No witnesses. Clean scene.

Too clean.

She made a mental note to follow up, then glanced at the man beside her. Detective Cole Rivas, her partner for the past two years, was scrolling through his phone with the practiced disinterest of someone who'd perfected the art of looking busy while doing nothing. Sharp jaw, perpetual five o'clock shadow, eyes that looked tired even after a full night's sleep.

"You paying attention?" Sienna asked, voice low.

"To what? The captain explaining why we can't afford new printers but somehow found money for a consultant?" Cole didn't look up from his phone. "I'm multitasking. It's a skill."

"Right."

"Besides, you're taking notes. I'll just copy yours later."

Captain Ortiz cleared his throat, signaling a shift in topic. He was a broad-shouldered man in his late forties with the kind of presence that filled a room without effort. Former beat cop, twenty years on the force. Sienna respected him. She just didn't always agree with him.

"Animal Welfare," Ortiz said, nodding toward Sienna. "You've got the floor."

Sienna straightened, flipped her notepad open. "Seventeen calls overnight. Most heat-related—dogs left in cars, animals without access to water, one rabbit left in a wire cage on a balcony in full sun. We responded to twelve. Five were resolved before we arrived."

"Resolved how?" Ortiz asked.

"Owners returned. Situations de-escalated. One case where a neighbor intervened." Sienna paused. "The Maple Street incident is worth noting. Locked car, overheated dog. By the time patrol arrived, the windows were cracked, the dog had water, and the owner was back. No signs of forced entry, but the owner didn't remember leaving the windows open that far."

Cole glanced at her. "You think someone broke in?"

"I think someone did something. The scene was too clean. No scratches on the lock, no broken glass, no damage. If it was a Good Samaritan, they knew what they were doing."

"Or the owner's lying. Covering their ass to avoid a citation."

"Maybe."

Ortiz leaned back in his chair, arms crossed. "You want to pursue it?"

Sienna hesitated. The honest answer was yes. The practical answer was that she had fourteen other cases on her desk, a court appearance scheduled for Thursday, and a system that didn't reward curiosity. "I want to log it. See if there's a pattern."

"Fair enough. Anything else?"

"The shelters are at capacity. The heatwave's driving up intake. I've been in contact with the city's animal control coordinator. They're asking for additional funding to extend hours and increase staffing, but—"

"But the budget's locked until next quarter," Ortiz finished. "I know. I've had the same conversation with the mayor's office three times this month."

"So what do we tell them?"

Ortiz's expression didn't change. "We tell them we're doing everything we can within our current resources."

"Which isn't enough."

"No," Ortiz agreed. "It's not."

One of the patrol supervisors—a veteran sergeant named Kowalski—spoke up from across the table. "What about volunteers? Can't we coordinate better with the nonprofits?"

"We're already coordinating," Sienna said. "The problem isn't manpower. It's capacity. You can't house fifty animals in a facility built for thirty."

"So we're back to funding," Kowalski said.

"We're always back to funding," Cole muttered.

Ortiz shot him a look but didn't disagree.

The room went quiet. Sienna felt the weight of it—the unspoken acknowledgment that they were all operating in a system designed to manage problems, not solve them.

ADA Clarence Lee spoke up from the far end of the table. He was younger than most, mid-thirties, with wire-rimmed glasses and the kind of precise diction that came from too many hours in courtrooms. "Detective Halbrook, regarding proactive measures—what exactly are you proposing?"

Sienna met his gaze. "Increased patrols in high-risk areas. Public awareness campaigns. Coordination with local vets and shelters to identify repeat offenders before situations escalate."

"All of which require funding we don't have," Lee said. Not unkindly. Just factually. "And legal standing we may not be able to justify. Animal welfare cases are notoriously difficult to prosecute unless there's clear evidence of intent and significant harm. You know this."

"I do."

"Then you understand why we have to prioritize cases with the highest likelihood of successful prosecution."

"I understand that we're letting people get away with cruelty because it's easier than fighting for convictions."

Lee's expression didn't shift. "I understand that you're frustrated. But the law has limits, Detective. We work within them, or we don't work at all."

Sienna didn't respond. Lee wasn't wrong. He was just operating in a different framework—one where success was measured in convictions, not lives saved.

Cole leaned back in his chair, arms folded. "You can't save them all, Halbrook."

She turned to look at him. "What?"

"You can't save them all. You know that, right? You can work every case, chase every lead, push every angle, and at the end of the day, some of them are still going to slip through. That's the job."

Sienna held his gaze, then looked away. "I know."

"Do you?"

She didn't answer.

Ortiz stood, signaling the end of the briefing. "All right. Everyone knows their assignments. Let's get to work."

The room emptied in a slow shuffle of chairs and murmured conversations. Sienna gathered her notes and headed for the door. Cole fell into step beside her, hands in his pockets.

"You're going to follow up on the Maple Street thing, aren't you?" he said.

"Probably."

"Even though it's a dead end."

"I don't know that it's a dead end."

"Halbrook." Cole stopped walking, turned to face her. "I've been doing this job long enough to know when someone's chasing a ghost. You've got a dozen active cases. You've got court on Thursday. And you're about to spend time and energy on a case where the victim is fine and the crime—if there even was one—left zero evidence."

"Your point?"

"My point is that you're good at this job. Better than most. But you're going to burn out if you keep trying to solve every mystery that doesn't add up." He paused. "And for the record, I'm not saying don't follow up. I'm saying pick your battles."

Sienna studied him. Cole had been a detective for twelve years, most of it in Vice before transferring to Animal Welfare after a case went sideways. He was good at the job because he knew when to care and when to let go.

"I'll keep that in mind," she said.

"Sure you will."

They walked the rest of the way to their shared office in silence. It was a small room on the third floor, barely big enough for two desks, a filing cabinet, and a dying pothos plant that Cole insisted on watering. Sienna dropped into her chair, opened her laptop, and pulled up the Maple Street incident report again.

Cole settled at his desk and started typing. After a minute, he spoke without looking up. "You really think someone broke into that car to save a dog?"

"I think someone did something. And I think they knew what they were doing."

"Why?"

"Because the lock wasn't damaged. The car wasn't scratched. The dog had water. Whoever did it wasn't panicking. They were methodical."

Cole stopped typing. "So what, you think we've got a vigilante locksmith running around saving animals?"

"I think we've got someone who cares more about the outcome than the law."

"That's called a criminal, Halbrook."

"Or a Good Samaritan."

"Same thing, depending on who you ask."

Sienna didn't respond. She was already pulling up the precinct's database, running a search for similar incidents over the past six months. Locked cars, animals in distress, resolved scenes with no clear explanation.

The search returned three results. Then five. Then eight.

She leaned back in her chair.

"Halbrook?" Cole's voice had lost its sardonic edge. "What'd you find?"

"A pattern," she said.

Cole wheeled his chair over, looked at her screen. His expression shifted—still skeptical, but interested now. "Eight incidents in six months. All clean scenes. All animals unharmed."

"All resolved before we arrived."

"Could be coincidence."

"Could be," Sienna agreed. "But I don't think it is."

Cole was quiet, then let out a long breath. "You're going to chase this, aren't you?"

"I'm going to log it. See where it goes."

"And if it goes nowhere?"

"Then I'll move on."

Cole didn't look convinced, but he didn't argue. He just rolled his chair back to his desk and resumed typing. After a minute, he spoke again. "For what it's worth, I hope you're right. About the Good Samaritan thing."

"Why?"

"Because if someone's out there doing what we can't, maybe the system's not as broken as I think it is."

Sienna didn't respond. She pulled up the Maple Street file again, opened a new document, and started typing.

Case File: Anomalous Animal Rescues

Incident Count: 8

Timeframe: 6 months

Pattern: Clean interventions, no forced entry, animals unharmed, no suspect identified.

Status: Under investigation.

Lead Detective: Halbrook, S.

Priority: Low (pending pattern confirmation)

She saved the file, closed her laptop. The office was small enough that she could see the water stain in the corner of the ceiling, the crooked blinds, the stack of case files that seemed to grow every week.

But somewhere in the noise, there was something else. A thread she couldn't quite see yet, but could feel pulling at her attention.

Cole glanced over. "You're doing that thing again."

"What thing?"

"The thing where you stare at nothing and mentally solve crimes."

"I'm not solving anything. I'm thinking."

"Same thing."

Sienna picked up her coffee. "You really think I'm wasting my time with this?"

Cole considered the question. "I think you're good at finding patterns other people miss. I also think you're going to drive yourself crazy if you chase every anomaly that crosses your desk." He paused. "But no. I don't think you're wasting your time. Not yet, anyway."

"High praise."

"I'm a realist, Halbrook. It's my job."

"What's my job?"

"Apparently, finding vigilante locksmiths."

Somewhere out there, someone was breaking the law to do the right thing. And Sienna Halbrook was going to find out who.

Chapter 3
Night Two

Kai told himself he wouldn't do it again.

He spent the entire day at Brennan's trying to convince himself that last night had been an anomaly—a one-time intervention born of impulse and proximity. The dog had been right there. The street had been empty. It didn't mean anything.

He'd worked through the morning sanding down a Victorian-era dresser, the repetitive motion giving his hands something to do while his mind circled the same questions. What if someone had seen him? What if the video ended up in the wrong hands? What if the next time, he wasn't so lucky?

His coworker Marcus had asked him twice if he was feeling okay. Kai had said he was fine. Marcus hadn't looked convinced.

By noon, Kai had almost believed his own rationalization.

By three, the rationalization started to crack.

By the time his shift ended at eight, the pulse was back.

It came while he was locking up the shop, a faint pressure at the base of his skull that sharpened as he turned onto the main road. Not panic this time. Distress—low-grade, persistent, the kind of fear that came from prolonged discomfort rather than immediate danger. Kai stopped walking, closed his eyes, and tried to tune it out.

The signal didn't fade.

He stood there for a full minute, hands in his pockets, jaw tight. He could go home. Make dinner. Pretend he didn't feel what he felt.

Or he could follow the signal.

Kai turned left instead of right and started walking.

The strip mall was three blocks away, a row of low-slung buildings with faded signage and half-empty parking lots. A laundromat, a check-cashing place, a dollar store with bars on the windows. The kind of neighborhood that looked tired even in daylight.

The pulse led him to the back lot, where a handful of vehicles sat scattered across cracked asphalt. One—a white panel van with rust along the wheel wells—wasn't empty.

Kai approached slowly, scanning for cameras. There was one mounted above the laundromat's back door, but the angle was wrong. He kept his head down, hood up, hands visible but relaxed.

The van's rear windows were tinted, but the driver's side had a narrow gap where the glass didn't quite meet the frame. Kai crouched beside it, peered inside. The interior was cluttered—cardboard boxes, loose tools, a tarp bunched in the corner. And in the back, pressed against the far wall, a cat.

Tabby, small and thin, with matted fur and wide eyes. The pulse intensified. Kai felt the animal's fear like a hand around his throat—tight, suffocating, laced with exhaustion. The van's interior was an oven. No ventilation. No water.

Kai's hands moved before his mind caught up.

He pulled the pick set from his jacket and worked the lock. The van was older, the mechanism simpler than the sedan from last night. The pins set quickly—one, two, three. The lock turned. He eased the door open.

The smell hit him. Urine, sweat, stale air. The cat didn't move. It just stared at him, trembling, too weak to do more than flatten its ears.

Kai reached into his other pocket and pulled out the collapsible water bottle. He'd refilled it this morning without thinking about why.

He poured water into the cap, set it on the floor near the cat. The animal's nose twitched. It leaned forward, hesitant, and lapped at the water with a desperation that made Kai's chest tight.

He refilled the cap twice more, watching the cat drink, feeling the pulse in his head ease with each swallow. The fear softened. Became manageable.

Kai cracked the rear windows, checked the door locks, then paused. Last night, he'd left the scene clean. No trace, no message. But something about that felt incomplete.

He pulled a pen from his pocket, found a scrap of receipt in his wallet, and wrote two words in block letters.

DO MORE.

He left the note on the dashboard, weighted down by the water bottle, then closed the door and tested the handle. Locked. No scratches. No evidence.

He stepped back, pulled his hood lower, and walked toward the edge of the lot.

The adrenaline hit halfway across—sharp, electric. His heart was pounding. His hands were steady.

He also felt something else. Something heavier.

Commitment.

Last night, he could have told himself it was a fluke. Tonight, he couldn't. Tonight, he'd gone looking for the signal. He'd followed it deliberately, knowing what he'd find, knowing what he'd do. That wasn't impulse. That was choice.

And choice meant responsibility.

He didn't know if that made him a good person or a criminal.

Maybe both.

Kai turned the corner and disappeared into the grid of residential streets, the pulse fading behind him.

· · ·

He didn't go home.

Instead, he walked. The city at night had a rhythm he'd learned to navigate. Quiet blocks where the only sound was the hum of air conditioners. Busier streets where late-night diners spilled light onto the sidewalk.

Kai moved through it all like a ghost.

He liked it that way. Anonymity was a kind of freedom. No one expected anything from him. No one asked questions.

His phone buzzed. He pulled it out, glanced at the screen. A text from his father.

You working tomorrow?

Kai stared at the message, then typed a reply.

Yeah. Morning shift.

The response came almost immediately.

Good. Stop by after. I'll make dinner.

Kai didn't respond. He pocketed the phone and kept walking.

His relationship with Liam had been strained since the accident. Not hostile, exactly. Just distant. Liam didn't understand what had changed in Kai, and Kai didn't know how to explain it. So they orbited each other carefully, avoiding the deeper questions neither of them wanted to answer.

The pulse came again.

This time, it was faint—distant enough that he could have ignored it if he wanted to. A dog, maybe. Somewhere east. Not urgent. Not yet.

Kai stopped walking. He stood in the middle of the sidewalk, hands in his pockets.

He could go home. Get some sleep.

Or he could turn east.

He turned east.

The signal led him to a residential block where the houses sat close together, separated by chain-link fences and narrow driveways. Most of the windows were dark. Kai moved slowly, scanning for the source.

He found it in a backyard three houses down—a dog chained to a post, lying on bare dirt with no shelter, no water, no shade. The chain was short, maybe six feet. The dog lifted its head as Kai approached the fence, ears flat, eyes wary.

The pulse sharpened. Fear, yes. But also resignation. The kind that came from knowing no one was coming to help.

Kai's hands tightened into fists.

This wasn't neglect born of ignorance. This was deliberate. Someone had put that chain there. Someone had decided this was acceptable.

The anger surprised him. It was sharp and immediate, cutting through the usual numbness he felt when the signals came. He'd learned to manage the empathy, to compartmentalize the fear and pain. But the anger was new.

And it felt dangerous.

The fence was locked, but the latch was simple. He glanced at the house—dark windows, no movement—then slipped the latch and stepped into the yard. The dog watched him but didn't bark. It just lay there, too tired or too defeated to react.

Kai crouched a few feet away, pulled out the water bottle, and poured water into the cap. He set it on the ground, then slid it forward slowly. The dog sniffed, hesitated, then drank.

Kai refilled the cap twice more, then stood and looked at the chain. It was padlocked to the post. He could pick it. He could free the dog, take it somewhere safe.

But then what? The dog would end up in a shelter already over capacity. The owner would get another animal. The cycle would continue.

Kai stared at the chain, then pulled out his pen and another scrap of paper.

DO MORE.

He left the note tucked under the water bottle, then slipped back through the fence and latched it behind him.

The pulse eased. The dog was still chained, still trapped, but it had water. It had a chance. And the owner had a message.

Kai walked away, hands in his pockets, hood up.

He didn't feel good about it. He didn't feel like a hero.

But he felt like he'd done something.

And for now, that was enough.

By the time Kai got home, it was past midnight. He dropped his jacket on the chair, kicked off his boots, and went straight to the bathroom sink. His reflection looked the same as it had the night before—tired, wired.

But something was different. He could see it in his eyes. A hardness that hadn't been there before. A certainty.

He'd crossed a line tonight. Not just by intervening again, but by choosing to. By actively seeking out the signals instead of waiting for them to find him.

And there was no going back.

He splashed cold water on his face, counted his breaths.

It didn't work.

He walked into the main room, dropped onto the futon, and pulled out his phone. He opened the notes app and added two new entries.

Strip mall. White van. Tabby. Dehydrated, overheated. Left water, note. No confrontation.

Residential. Backyard chain. Dog. Chronic neglect. Left water, note. No confrontation.

He stared at the entries, then scrolled up through the list. Sixteen rescues now. Two in one night.

He closed the app and set the phone on the floor.

The rain had stopped. The city was quiet. Somewhere out there, more signals waited.

Kai closed his eyes.
He couldn't sleep.
An hour later, he was walking again.

Chapter 4
Viral Ghost

Mina Torres lived in the kind of apartment that looked better in photos than in person. Exposed brick that was actually just painted drywall. Industrial lighting from a big-box store. A desk from Craigslist she pretended was vintage. The aesthetic was "urban journalist," which was another way of saying "broke but aspirational."

She sat at the desk now, laptop open, coffee going cold in a chipped mug. The cursor blinked at her. She'd been staring at it for twenty minutes.

This was the part of journalism no one talked about—the paralysis that came before the words. Mina had been freelancing for *The Signal Line* for two years, churning out local news, op-eds, investigative pieces that got buried under clickbait about celebrity scandals.

She was good at her job. But "good" didn't pay the rent. "good" didn't get you noticed.

What she needed was a story that broke through the noise.

And now, sitting in her apartment at 2 a.m., she thought she might have found it.

The video sat in her downloads folder, sent to her an hour ago by

Mrs. Delgado—a retired teacher on Maple Street who filmed anything unusual in her neighborhood. Most of the time, it was nothing. A suspicious van. A loud argument. Once, a raccoon in someone's trash.

This time, it was something else.

Mina clicked play for the fifth time.

The footage was grainy, shot through a second-floor window at night, but the streetlight provided just enough illumination. A hooded figure approached a parked car, crouched beside the driver's door, and worked the lock with practiced efficiency. No fumbling. No hesitation. The door opened. The figure reached inside, stayed there for maybe thirty seconds, then closed the door and walked away.

Clean. Precise. Gone.

The timestamp said 12:23 a.m. Mrs. Delgado's notes said the car belonged to someone who'd left their dog inside while they ate dinner two blocks away. By the time the owner returned, the dog was fine. The windows were cracked. There was water in the car.

No damage. No theft. Just a rescue.

Mina leaned back, chewing her pen. This was a story. The kind that didn't just get clicks—it got shared. It got talked about.

But it was also unverified. One video from one source. No police report. No official statement. No confirmation that the person in the video was actually helping the dog and not casing the car.

Journalism 101: verify before you publish. Get multiple sources. Confirm the facts.

But Journalism 2025: publish fast or someone else will.

Mina hated that she was even considering the second option. She'd gone into journalism because she believed in truth, in accountability. But the industry had changed. And if she wanted to survive, she had to change too.

Her phone buzzed. A text from her editor.

Got anything for tomorrow's morning post? Need 500 words by 8 a.m.

Mina stared at the message, then at the video, then at the blank document.

She thought about Mrs. Delgado, who'd sent her the footage because she trusted Mina to do something meaningful with it. She thought about the dog in the car, who would have died if no one had intervened. She thought about the hooded figure who'd risked arrest to do what was right.

And she thought about the system that had made that risk necessary.

She started typing.

The Ghost Who Saved a Dog

By Mina Torres

Late Tuesday night, on a quiet residential street, something unusual happened. A dog—left alone in a locked car during a summer heatwave—was rescued. Not by police. Not by animal control. But by someone the owner never saw.

Security footage obtained by *The Signal Line* shows a hooded figure approaching the vehicle just after midnight. Within seconds, the car door is unlocked. The figure reaches inside, provides water to the distressed animal, cracks the windows for ventilation, then locks the car again and disappears into the night.

No damage. No theft. No confrontation.

Just a rescue.

The owner, who declined to be named, returned to find their dog alive and well—and no explanation for how the situation had been resolved. Police were not called. No charges were filed.

But the question remains: Who was the rescuer? And why?

Sources close to the investigation suggest this may not be an isolated incident. Similar reports have surfaced over the past six months—animals in distress, mysteriously aided by an unknown individual who leaves no trace. Some have begun calling this person "the Ghost."

The Ghost doesn't ask for recognition. Doesn't wait for thanks. Doesn't operate within the bounds of the law.

But in a city where animal welfare resources are stretched thin and emergency response times can mean the difference between life and death, the Ghost is doing what the system can't—or won't.

Is this vigilante justice? Or is it something else?

One thing is certain: someone out there is watching. And when the law fails, they act.

The question now is whether the city will stop them—or start asking why they're necessary in the first place.

Mina read through the draft twice, made a few edits, then hit send. The article posted at 6:47 a.m. She closed her laptop, drained the last of her cold coffee, and went to bed.

By the time she woke up four hours later, the story had 12,000 views.

By noon, it had 50,000.

By the end of the day, it was everywhere.

Mina sat at a coffee shop downtown, scrolling through the comments section. She'd come here to escape her apartment, but also because she wanted to see how people were reacting in real time.

And they were all talking about the Ghost.

She'd overheard three separate conversations in the past hour. College students debating whether vigilante justice was ever justified. A couple arguing about whether the person in the video was a hero or a criminal. An older man telling the barista that "someone finally had the guts to do what needed to be done."

The reactions split into three camps.

Camp One: The Romantics

"This is what a hero looks like. Not a cop. Not a politician. Just someone who cares."

"I hope they never catch the Ghost. We need more people like this."

Camp Two: The Skeptics

"Breaking into someone's car is still a crime. What if they got the wrong vehicle?"

"How do we know this person isn't using 'rescue' as a cover for theft?"

Camp Three: The Pragmatists

"I don't care if it's legal. That dog would've died if no one intervened."

"The system is broken. If this is what it takes to fix it, so be it."

Mina kept scrolling. The story had been picked up by two local TV stations, a regional news aggregator, and dozens of social media accounts. The video had been shared thousands of times.

The Ghost had become a phenomenon.

And Mina had started it.

Her phone buzzed. Another text from her editor.

Great work. Follow-up piece tomorrow? Interview with police? Public reaction angle?

Mina typed a quick reply.

On it.

She opened a new note and started brainstorming. The story had legs. She could go investigative—dig into the pattern of rescues, try to identify the Ghost. Or human interest—interview people who'd been helped, explore the systemic failures that made someone like the Ghost necessary.

Or she could do both.

Her phone buzzed again. An email. Subject line: **Re: Ghost Rescuer Article**.

Mina opened it.

Ms. Torres,

I read your article this morning. I think I've encountered the Ghost before. Three months ago, my cat was trapped in my garage overnight. I didn't realize it until the next morning, and by then, someone had already gotten her out. The side door was unlocked—I know I'd locked it the night before—and there was a bowl of water on the floor. No note. No explanation.

I thought it was strange, but I didn't report it. After reading your article, I'm not so sure.

—Angela R.

Mina read the email twice, then forwarded it to a folder labeled **Ghost Follow-Up**. She opened her inbox and found three more messages with similar subject lines. All from people who thought they'd been helped by the Ghost. All with stories that fit the pattern.

She leaned back in her chair.

This wasn't just a story anymore. This was a movement.

And Mina Torres was at the center of it.

Detective Sienna Halbrook saw the article at 3:47 p.m., sitting in her car outside the precinct. She'd been scrolling through her phone when the headline caught her eye.

The Ghost Who Saved a Dog

She clicked the link, read the article, watched the video.

Then she sat in silence for a full minute.

The figure in the footage matched the profile she'd been building. Clean intervention. No forced entry. Methodical. Efficient. The same pattern she'd logged in her case file.

But now it wasn't just a pattern. It was public.

Sienna closed the article, opened her contacts, and called Cole.

He picked up on the second ring. "Halbrook. Please tell me you're not calling to give me more work."

"Have you seen the article?"

"What article?"

"The one about the Ghost."

A pause. "The what?"

"Check *The Signal Line*. Front page."

She heard typing, then a low whistle. "Well. That's not good."

"No. It's not."

"You think it's the same person?"

"I know it is."

Another pause. "So what do we do?"

Sienna stared at the precinct building. "I don't know yet."

"You want my advice?"

"Not really."

"I'm going to give it anyway. This just became a public case. Which means Ortiz is going to want answers. Fast."

"I know."

"And if you don't close it, someone else will. And they won't care about the nuance."

Sienna didn't respond. Cole was right. The moment the Ghost became a media story, the rules changed. It wasn't about justice anymore. It was about optics.

"I'll see you tomorrow," she said.

"Halbrook—"

She hung up.

She sat in the car, phone in her lap. Then she opened the article again.

The Ghost doesn't ask for recognition. Doesn't wait for thanks. Doesn't operate within the bounds of the law.

But in a city where animal welfare resources are stretched thin, the Ghost is doing what the system can't—or won't.

Sienna closed the article, started the car, and drove home.

Kai saw the article at 9:32 p.m., lying on his futon with his phone in his hand. He'd been scrolling aimlessly when the headline appeared in his feed.

The Ghost Who Saved a Dog

He clicked the link. Read the article. Watched the video.

His chest tightened.

That was him. On camera. Identifiable, maybe, if someone looked close enough. The footage was grainy, but the streetlight had been bright. His build, his gait, the way he moved—it was all there.

He'd been so careful. He'd checked for cameras. He'd kept his head down, his hood up.

But shadows could be captured. And now his shadow had a name.

The Ghost.

He read the article again, slower, paying attention to the details. The tone was sympathetic. Almost admiring. The comments were mixed, but the overall sentiment was clear: people were paying attention.

The Ghost had a name now. A myth. A story.

Part of him wanted to disappear. Delete his notes, stop following the signals, go back to being invisible. The attention was dangerous. The more people talked, the more likely someone would figure out who he was.

But another part of him—the part that had left the note saying **DO MORE**—felt something else.

Validation, maybe. Or purpose.

Because the article was right. The system wasn't working. The shelters were full. The response times were too slow. And someone had to do something.

Kai set his phone down, closed his eyes, and listened to the pulse in his head.

It was still there. Waiting.

He stood up, pulled on his jacket, and reached for his boots.

The Ghost had a name now.

He wasn't a story anymore. The Ghost was a schedule.

Chapter 5
The Task Force Briefing

The briefing room was more crowded than usual. Sienna counted fourteen people as she walked in—detectives, patrol supervisors, a representative from animal control, and two faces she didn't recognize but assumed were from the mayor's office based on their suits and the way they stood near the back with their arms crossed. Captain Ortiz was at the front, setting up a laptop connected to the projector. ADA Clarence Lee sat in the front row, tablet in hand, already looking impatient.

Cole slid into the seat next to Sienna, coffee in hand. "This is going to be a disaster."

"You don't know that."

"I know that when the mayor's office shows up to a briefing about a viral video, it's not because they care about animal welfare. It's because they care about optics."

Sienna didn't argue.

Ortiz cleared his throat, and the room quieted. "All right, let's get started." He clicked the laptop, and the projector screen lit up with a still frame from Mrs. Delgado's video—the hooded figure crouched beside the car, hands working the lock.

"As most of you are aware, a video surfaced yesterday showing an unidentified individual breaking into a vehicle to rescue a dog left in a hot car. The video was posted by *The Signal Line*, has since gone viral, and as of this morning has been viewed over two hundred thousand times."

One of the patrol supervisors raised a hand. "Do we have an ID on the suspect?"

"Not yet. The footage is too grainy for facial recognition, and the individual kept their hood up. We're working with the tech unit to enhance the video."

"What about the car owner? Did they file a report?"

"No. The owner declined to press charges. They claim the dog was fine and they don't want to pursue the matter."

Cole leaned over to Sienna. "Of course they don't. Because they know they'd look like the bad guy."

Ortiz clicked to the next slide—a map of the city with eight red pins scattered across the west and north sides. "This isn't an isolated incident. Detective Halbrook has been tracking similar cases over the past six months. Eight confirmed interventions, all involving animals in distress, all resolved before we arrived on scene. No forced entry. No theft. No violence. Just clean rescues."

The room murmured. Sienna felt the weight of attention shift toward her.

"Detective Halbrook," Ortiz said, nodding in her direction. "You want to walk us through the pattern?"

Sienna stood, moved to the front, and took the clicker from Ortiz. She advanced to the next slide—a table summarizing the incidents.

"Eight cases over six months. Locations vary, but they're all within a five-mile radius of the west side. Victims include dogs, cats, and one rabbit. Methods vary slightly, but the common thread is precision. No damage to property. No confrontation with owners. In three cases, the individual left water for the animal. In two cases, they left notes."

"What kind of notes?" one of the detectives asked.

Sienna clicked to the next slide. A photo of a scrap of paper with two words in block letters: **DO MORE.**

The room went quiet.

"That's it?" someone said. "Just 'do more'?"

"That's it. Short. Direct. Left at the scene for the owner to find."

ADA Lee spoke up from the front row. "Do we have handwriting analysis?"

"We do. But it's inconclusive. Block letters, written with a ball-point pen. No distinctive markers."

Lee made a note on his tablet. "What about surveillance footage from the other incidents?"

"Limited. Most of the locations don't have cameras, or the angles don't capture the individual clearly. The Maple Street video is the best we have."

Ortiz stepped forward. "Which brings us to the reason we're all here. The mayor's office has made it clear that this case is now a priority. The video has generated significant public interest, and we're under pressure to respond."

One of the suits from the back spoke up. "The mayor is concerned about the message this sends. If the public perceives that vigilante action is acceptable—or worse, heroic—we risk encouraging copycats. That's a liability issue, both legally and politically."

Cole muttered under his breath. "There it is."

Sienna shot him a look.

The suit continued. "We need to identify this individual, bring them in, and make it clear that breaking the law—even with good intentions—has consequences."

"Understood," Ortiz said. He turned back to the room. "Effective immediately, Detective Halbrook and Detective Rivas will head up a task force dedicated to identifying and apprehending the individual known as 'the Ghost.' You'll have access to tech support, additional patrol resources, and coordination with animal control. I want daily updates and a clear plan of action by the end of the week."

Sienna felt her stomach tighten. A task force. For a case that, until yesterday, had been a low-priority anomaly.

Cole raised his hand. "Captain, with all due respect, is this really the best use of resources? We've got active cases—abuse, neglect, trafficking. This person hasn't hurt anyone. They've helped animals. Shouldn't we be focusing on actual criminals?"

The room shifted uncomfortably.

Ortiz's expression didn't change. "I understand your concern, Detective. But the decision has been made."

"Because of optics," Cole said.

"Because of public safety," Lee said. "Vigilantism, no matter how well-intentioned, undermines the rule of law. If we allow this to continue unchecked, we set a precedent that individuals can take justice into their own hands. That's not a precedent we can afford."

Cole opened his mouth to respond, but Sienna put a hand on his arm. He glanced at her, then sat back, jaw tight.

Ortiz clicked to the next slide—a list of action items. "Tech unit will continue working on video enhancement. Patrol will increase presence in the target area. Animal control will coordinate with shelters and vets. And Detectives Halbrook and Rivas will lead the investigative effort—interviews, pattern analysis, and suspect profiling."

He paused, looking around the room. "I know this isn't a typical case. But it's the one we've been given. Let's do it right."

The briefing ended ten minutes later. Sienna stayed at the front, staring at the map on the screen—the eight red pins marking the Ghost's interventions.

Cole walked up beside her. "You okay?"

"I don't know."

"You don't have to like this, you know. It's a PR stunt. Ortiz knows it. We all know it."

"That doesn't change the fact that we have to do it."

"No. But it does change how we do it."

Sienna turned to look at him. "What do you mean?"

"I mean we can go through the motions, file the reports, keep the mayor's office happy. Or we can actually try to figure out who this person is and why they're doing it." He paused. "The question is, which one do you want to do?"

Sienna looked back at the map. Eight interventions. Eight animals saved. Zero harm done.

"I want to understand," she said.

"Understand what?"

"Why someone would risk arrest to save a dog."

Cole studied her, then nodded. "All right. Then let's understand."

Sienna spent the rest of the morning in her office, building a profile. She pulled up the case files, cross-referenced the locations, and started mapping the timeline. The first intervention had been six months ago—a cat trapped in a garage. The most recent had been three nights ago—the dog in the car on Maple Street.

The frequency had increased. One intervention in the first month. Two in the second. Three in the third. The Ghost was getting more active. More confident.

Or more desperate.

She opened a new document and started typing.

Profile: The Ghost

Demographics: Unknown. Likely male based on build. Age 20-40. Physically fit.

Skills: Lockpicking. Surveillance evasion. Animal handling. Suggests prior training—possibly locksmith, security, or related field.

Motivation: Driven by empathy for animals in distress. No evidence of financial gain. Interventions are targeted and precise, suggesting a moral framework rather than opportunism.

Behavior Pattern: Operates at night. Avoids confrontation. Leaves no trace. In some cases, leaves notes with "DO MORE," suggesting a desire to provoke change.

Risk Assessment: Low. No evidence of violence or intent to harm.

She read through the profile twice, then leaned back in her chair. It was a start. But it didn't answer the question that kept nagging at her.

Why?

Why risk everything for animals most people wouldn't even notice? Why operate in the shadows instead of working within the system?

Her phone buzzed. A text from Cole.

Got something. Meet me in the conference room.

Sienna grabbed her tablet and headed down the hall.

Cole was standing in front of a whiteboard when she walked in, marker in hand. He'd drawn a rough map of the city and marked the eight intervention sites with red circles.

"Look at this," he said, tapping the board. "All eight incidents are within a five-mile radius. Most clustered in two neighborhoods—west side residential and the industrial area near the strip mall."

Sienna studied the map. "So the Ghost lives or works in one of those areas."

"Probably. But here's the interesting part." Cole drew a line connecting the sites. "The interventions aren't random. They follow a pattern. The first few were opportunistic—animals in immediate danger. But the more recent ones are different. They're targeted."

"Targeted how?"

"Look at the timeline." Cole pointed to the dates. "The last three interventions happened within a week of each other. And all three involved chronic neglect, not acute emergencies. The dog chained in the backyard. The cat in the van. The rabbit on the balcony. These aren't situations the Ghost stumbled across. These are situations the Ghost went looking for."

Sienna felt a chill. "So the Ghost is escalating."

"Or evolving. From reactive to proactive. From rescuer to vigilante."

Sienna stared at the map. If Cole was right—if the Ghost was actively seeking out cases—then this wasn't just about saving animals. It was about making a statement.

DO MORE.

Not a plea. A challenge.

"We need to figure out how the Ghost is finding these cases," Sienna said. "They have to have a system."

"Agreed. But what kind?"

Sienna thought for a moment. "What if they're monitoring 911 calls? Or social media? People post about animal abuse all the time. Maybe the Ghost is tracking those reports and following up when the system doesn't."

Cole nodded slowly. "That would explain the targeting. And it would mean the Ghost has access to information most people don't."

"Or they're just paying attention," Sienna said. "Which is more than most people do."

Cole looked at her. "You sound like you admire them."

"I don't admire breaking the law. But I understand the frustration."

"Careful, Halbrook. That's a slippery slope."

"I know."

They stood in silence.

"So what's our next move?" Cole asked.

Sienna pulled out her phone, scrolled to a name she hadn't called in months. Dr. Haru Inoue, the city's veterinary pathologist. If anyone had insight into the animal welfare underground, it was him.

"We talk to people who care," Sienna said. "And we figure out who cares enough to break the law."

Cole raised an eyebrow. "You think the vet community knows who the Ghost is?"

"I think they might know someone who knows." She hit the call button. "And right now, theories are all we've got."

The phone rang twice before Haru picked up.

"Detective Halbrook," he said, his voice warm but cautious. "It's been a while."

"It has. I need your help with something."

"Let me guess. The Ghost Rescuer."

Sienna blinked. "You've heard about it."

"Everyone's heard about it. It's all anyone in the animal welfare community is talking about." He paused. "What do you want to know?"

"I want to know if anyone in your network has any idea who this person might be."

There was a long silence on the other end.

"Haru?"

"I'll see what I can find out. But Sienna—be careful. A lot of people in this community see the Ghost as a hero. If you're planning to arrest them, you're not going to make any friends."

"I'm not planning to arrest anyone. I'm planning to understand."

"Good," Haru said. "Because understanding is what we need more of."

He hung up.

Sienna lowered the phone, staring at the map on the whiteboard.

Somewhere out there, the Ghost was watching. Waiting. Planning the next rescue.

And Sienna Halbrook was going to find them.

Even if she wasn't sure what she'd do when she did.

Chapter 6
Ghost Debates

The rooftop was Kai's favorite place in the building. Not because it was beautiful—it wasn't. Just tar paper and gravel, a rusted air conditioning unit, and a low wall that separated the edge from a four-story drop. But it was quiet. Private.

He sat with his back against the wall, legs stretched out, phone in his hand. The night was warm, the air thick with the smell of asphalt and distant rain. Below, the city hummed with its usual noise—traffic, voices, the occasional siren. Above, the sky was a dull orange glow, too much light pollution to see stars.

Kai had read Mina's article three times now. Each time, the words felt heavier.

The Ghost doesn't ask for recognition. Doesn't wait for thanks. Doesn't operate within the bounds of the law.

But in a city where animal welfare resources are stretched thin and emergency response times can mean the difference between life and death, the Ghost is doing what the system can't—or won't.

He set the phone down, closed his eyes.

He had a name now. Not his real name, but a name nonetheless. The Ghost. Names had power. Names made things real. And now, instead of being an anonymous figure doing quiet work in the shadows, he was a story. A myth. A symbol.

And symbols got hunted.

He thought about the video. He'd watched it twice, studying the footage the way a detective might. His posture. His movements. The way he crouched beside the car, worked the lock, moved with purpose. It was him, unmistakably, but also not him. The camera had turned him into something abstract. A silhouette. A ghost.

The comments on the article had been split. Half the people thought he was a hero. The other half thought he was a criminal. A few thought he was both.

Kai wasn't sure which camp he belonged to.

But the world didn't deal in nuance. You were either good or bad, legal or illegal, right or wrong. There was no category for "person who breaks the law because the law is failing."

Except maybe vigilante.

And vigilantes, historically, didn't end well.

He pulled his knees up, rested his arms on them. Somewhere out there, the police were looking for him. He didn't know how seriously they were taking it, but he knew they were looking. The article had made sure of that.

The smart thing to do would be to stop. Delete his notes. Throw away the pick set. Go back to being a locksmith who minded his own business and ignored the signals. Let the Ghost fade into obscurity.

But the signals wouldn't stop. They never did.

And neither would the suffering.

Kai pulled out his phone again, opened the notes app, and scrolled through the list. Eighteen rescues now. Eighteen animals that would have died or suffered if he hadn't intervened. Eighteen moments where the system had failed and he'd stepped in to fill the gap.

DO MORE.

He'd written those words on a scrap of paper and left them for strangers to find. At the time, it had felt like a challenge—a way to make people confront their own negligence. But now, reading Mina's article, he realized the words had become something else.

A motto. A mission statement.

And maybe, a promise.

Kai stood, walked to the edge of the roof, and looked down at the street below. A few people walked past, heads down, oblivious. A car turned the corner, headlights cutting through the dark.

From up here, the city looked almost peaceful. The noise was muted, the chaos reduced to patterns of light and movement. But Kai knew better. Down there, in the spaces between the streetlights, animals were suffering. Trapped in cars. Chained in yards. Locked in cages. Forgotten.

And the people who were supposed to help—the shelters, the police, the system—were overwhelmed, underfunded, or simply didn't care enough.

That was the truth Mina's article had danced around but never quite said. The Ghost existed because the system had failed. And as long as the system kept failing, the Ghost would keep existing.

The question was whether Kai was willing to be that Ghost.

He thought about what it would mean to keep going. Not just reacting to signals as they came, but actively seeking them out. Planning. Preparing.

The idea scared him. It meant accepting that this wasn't temporary. It meant accepting the risk of arrest, exposure, and everything that came with it.

But the alternative—doing nothing—felt like a betrayal.

He pulled out his phone and opened a new note.

Next Steps:

1. Study patrol routes. Know where police are likely to be and when.

2. Upgrade tools. Faster picks. Better flashlight. Portable water containers.

3. Map high-risk areas. Shelters, known abusers, repeat offenders.

4. Minimize exposure. No more mistakes. No more cameras.

He stared at the list, then added one more line.

5. Accept that this is who I am now.

He saved the note, pocketed the phone, and walked back to the center of the roof.

The pulse was there, faint but persistent. Somewhere east. Not urgent, but present. A reminder that the work was never done.

Kai took a breath, let it out slowly, and made his decision.

He wasn't going to stop.

He was going to get better.

The next morning, Kai walked into Brennan's with a plan. He clocked in, grabbed his apron, and headed to the back room. Marcus was already there, sanding down a chair leg, headphones in.

Kai pulled out his phone and opened a browser. He'd spent the past hour researching lock mechanisms—the kinds used in vehicles and residential gates. Most were standard pin tumblers, easy enough to pick with the right tools. But some of the newer models had security features that made them trickier. Anti-pick pins. Sidebar mechanisms. Electronic overrides.

He needed to be ready for all of them.

He pulled up a supplier website and started browsing. Tension wrenches in different sizes. Hook picks with finer tips. A bump key set. A small LED penlight that wouldn't draw attention. He added items to the cart, calculated the cost, and winced. It was more than he wanted to spend, but less than getting caught would cost him.

He checked out, selected expedited shipping, and closed the browser.

Marcus pulled out one earbud. "You good, man? You've been on your phone for like ten minutes."

"Yeah," Kai said. "Just ordering some tools."

"For here?"

"For a side project."

Marcus nodded, put the earbud back in, and went back to sanding.

That night, Kai spread a map of the city across his kitchen table. He'd printed it from an online source, marked it with the locations of his previous rescues, and started adding new data. Shelter addresses. Animal control response zones. Known problem areas flagged by online forums and social media posts.

He'd spent the afternoon combing through neighborhood Facebook groups, NextDoor posts, and Reddit threads. People complained about animal neglect all the time—dogs left outside in extreme weather, cats trapped in abandoned buildings, reports of hoarding situations. Most of the complaints went nowhere. The system was too slow, too overwhelmed, too bureaucratic.

But Kai could be fast. He could be decisive. He could fill the gaps.

The pattern was clearer now. Most of the signals he'd followed had come from two neighborhoods—the west side residential area where he lived, and the industrial zone near the strip mall. Both areas had high rates of animal neglect, low police presence, and limited access to resources.

He cross-referenced the online complaints with his own map, looking for overlap. Three locations stood out—places where multiple people had reported problems, where the system had failed to respond, where animals were still suffering.

He pulled out a red marker and circled them. A house on the edge of the industrial zone where neighbors had reported a dog left outside in all weather. A storage facility where someone had posted about hearing cats crying from inside a locked unit. An apartment complex where multiple residents had complained about a tenant hoarding animals.

Three targets. Three opportunities to intervene before the situations became emergencies.

Kai stared at the map, feeling the weight of what he was planning. This wasn't reactive anymore. This was deliberate. Calculated.

But what else was there? The system wasn't going to fix itself. The shelters were full. The response times were too slow. And the animals—the ones who couldn't speak, couldn't advocate, couldn't escape—were the ones who paid the price.

DO MORE.

Kai folded the map, tucked it into a drawer, and pulled out his notebook. He started sketching lock mechanisms from memory, practicing the mental choreography of picking them. Pin by pin. Tumbler by tumbler. The rhythm of it was soothing, almost meditative.

His phone buzzed. A text from his father.

You coming by this weekend?

Kai stared at the message, then typed a reply.

Maybe. I'll let you know.

He set the phone down and went back to sketching.

The pulse came again just after midnight. Kai was lying on the futon, half-asleep, when the sensation hit—sharp, insistent, threaded with panic. He sat up, pulled on his boots, and grabbed his jacket.

The new tools had arrived that afternoon. He'd spent an hour organizing them into a compact kit that fit in his inside pocket—tension wrenches, picks, a penlight, a collapsible water bottle, and a small first-aid kit. Everything he needed, nothing he didn't.

He checked his phone. The patrol schedule he'd pulled from a public records request showed that the west side had minimal coverage between midnight and two a.m. If he moved fast, he could follow the signal, intervene, and be gone before anyone noticed.

Kai pulled his hood up, pocketed the kit, and stepped outside.

The night was cooler than the previous few, the air carrying the faint smell of rain. He walked quickly, following the pulse as it sharpened. A dog. Close by. Trapped.

He found it ten minutes later—a small terrier locked in a fenced yard behind a duplex. The gate was padlocked, the dog pacing back and forth, whining. No water. No shelter. Just bare dirt and a chain-link fence.

Kai approached the gate, scanned for cameras, and found none. He pulled out the pick set, selected the tools he needed, and worked the padlock. It was a cheap model, easy to bypass. The lock clicked open in under thirty seconds.

He eased the gate open, stepped inside, and crouched low. The dog approached cautiously, ears flat, tail tucked. Kai held out his hand, let the animal sniff, then poured water into the cap of his bottle. The dog drank eagerly, the pulse in Kai's head easing with each swallow.

He refilled the cap twice more, then pulled out a scrap of paper and a pen.

DO MORE.

He left the note on the ground, weighted down by a rock, then slipped back through the gate and locked it behind him.

The pulse faded. The dog was still trapped, but it had water. It had a chance.

And the owner had a message.

Kai walked away, hands in his pockets, hood up.

Behind him, the city slept.

Ahead, more signals waited.

And the Ghost kept moving.

By the time Kai got home, it was nearly two a.m. He dropped his jacket on the chair, kicked off his boots, and went straight to the bathroom sink. His reflection stared back at him—tired, wired, caught between exhaustion and purpose.

He splashed cold water on his face, counted his breaths.

It didn't work. It never did.

But tonight, the noise felt different. Less like chaos and more like clarity.

He walked into the main room, pulled out his notebook, and added a new entry.

Duplex. Fenced yard. Terrier. Chronic neglect. Left water, note. No confrontation.

Nineteen rescues now.

He closed the notebook, set it on the table.

Three more targets. Three more opportunities.

The Ghost had work to do.

And Kai DuMoire was ready.

Chapter 7
The First Lead

The digital forensics lab was in the basement of the precinct, tucked between the evidence locker and the break room no one used. It was a small space—four workstations, a wall of monitors, and the perpetual hum of cooling fans. The air smelled like burnt coffee and electronics.

Sienna pushed through the door, Cole trailing behind her. Tommy Chen, the department's lead forensic analyst, looked up from his screen and waved them over. He was in his late twenties, perpetually tired, and the kind of person who could make a computer do things that seemed like magic. He lived on energy drinks and takeout.

"Detective Halbrook," Tommy said, spinning his chair to face them. "Right on time."

Sienna pulled up the empty chair beside him. "Let me guess. You're here to tell me the Ghost is actually three raccoons in a trench coat."

Tommy grinned. "Close. But no."

"What do you have?"

"Word travels fast," Tommy said. "It's a viral video about a vigilante animal rescuer. Half the department thinks it's a waste of time.

The other half thinks it's the best thing that's happened to this city in years." He pulled up a file on his screen. "For the record, I'm in the second camp."

Cole raised an eyebrow. "You think vigilantism is good for the city?"

"I think someone doing what we can't is better than no one doing anything at all." Tommy clicked through to the video. "But that's above my pay grade. You want the technical breakdown or the philosophical debate?"

"Technical," Sienna said.

Tommy pulled up the footage from Mrs. Delgado's phone. "I've been going through this frame by frame. Bad news first: the footage is grainy, the lighting is terrible, and the angle is wrong for facial recognition. Even with enhancement, we're not getting an ID from this."

"And the good news?" Sienna asked.

Tommy clicked through a series of stills, each one showing the hooded figure from a slightly different angle. "Good news: whoever this person is, they're methodical. Look at the posture. The way they approach the car. The tool selection. This isn't someone panicking or improvising. This is someone who knows what they're doing."

Sienna studied the images. Tommy was right. The figure moved with precision—no wasted motion, no hesitation.

"Can you tell anything about the tools?" she asked.

Tommy zoomed in on one of the frames. The figure's hands were visible, holding something small and metallic. "Lockpicking tools. Probably a tension wrench and a hook pick, based on the shape. Professional-grade, not the cheap stuff you buy online."

"So we're looking for someone with locksmith training," Cole said.

"Or someone who's really good at YouTube tutorials. But yeah, my money's on professional training. The speed, the technique—it's textbook."

Sienna made a note on her tablet. "What about the surrounding area? Any other cameras?"

Tommy grinned. "That's why I called you down here." He pulled up a map on the screen, marked with red dots. "I pulled footage from every camera within a three-block radius. Most are residential door-bell cams, but there are a few traffic cameras and one ATM camera that covers the corner of Maple and Fifth."

He clicked on one of the dots, and a new video window opened. Black-and-white footage, shot from a high angle, showing the inter-section. The timestamp matched the night of the rescue.

"Watch this," Tommy said, hitting play.

The video showed an empty street. A few cars passed. Then, at 12:19 a.m., a figure appeared at the edge of the frame—hooded, hands in pockets, walking with purpose. They turned onto Maple Street and disappeared from view.

"That's four minutes before the rescue," Tommy said. "And here's the kicker." He fast-forwarded to 12:31 a.m. The same figure reappeared, walking in the opposite direction. Same posture. Same gait. But this time, something was different.

Tommy paused the video and zoomed in. "Look at the jacket."

Sienna leaned closer. The figure's jacket had a slight bulge on the right side, near the hip. It hadn't been there in the earlier footage.

"Tool case," Tommy said. "Small, probably leather or canvas. The kind locksmiths use to carry picks and wrenches."

Sienna felt her pulse quicken. "Can you measure the dimensions?"

Tommy clicked through a few menus, overlaying a measurement grid on the image. "Roughly six by four inches. Compact. Profession-al." He pulled up a reference image—a standard locksmith's pick case. "This is what we're looking at. Not the cheap stuff. The real deal."

Cole whistled low. "So our Ghost is either a locksmith, or they trained with one."

"Or they're self-taught and really committed," Tommy said. "But yeah, this isn't amateur hour."

Sienna studied the figure. The way they moved. The way they

47

carried themselves. Not just competent, but practiced. Like someone who'd done this before and knew exactly how to avoid being seen.

"You know what's interesting?" Tommy said. "People call us after the dog's already dead. After the cat's been trapped for days. We're the cleanup crew, not the prevention team." He gestured at the screen. "Whoever this is—they're beating the system. They're getting there first. And honestly? I respect that."

Sienna looked at him. "You know we're supposed to arrest them, right?"

"I know. Doesn't mean I have to like it."

"Can you pull up the other incidents?" Sienna asked. "The ones from my case file. See if any of them have similar footage."

Tommy nodded, already typing. "Give me a few hours. I'll run a search for any cameras in the vicinity of those locations."

"Thanks, Tommy."

"No problem. This is the most interesting case I've worked in months." He glanced at her. "For what it's worth, I don't think this person is dangerous. I think they're just trying to help."

"Helping doesn't make it legal," Cole said.

"No," Tommy agreed. "But it makes it complicated."

Sienna and Cole walked back upstairs in silence. When they reached their office, Sienna dropped into her chair and opened her laptop. Cole sat across from her, watching her with the kind of patience that came from years of partnership.

"You're thinking," he said.

"I'm always thinking."

"You're thinking something specific. I can tell."

Sienna looked up. "Tommy's right. This person isn't dangerous. They're not stealing. They're not hurting anyone. They're just... filling a gap."

"A gap the system should be filling," Cole said.

"Exactly."

"So what do we do?"

Sienna leaned back in her chair. "We do our job. We investigate. We follow the leads. And when we find them, we figure out what comes next."

"And if what comes next is arresting someone who's saving animals?"

"Then we deal with it."

Cole didn't look convinced. "You know Ortiz is going to want results. And the mayor's office is going to want a conviction."

"I know."

"So what's the plan?"

Sienna pulled up the case file on her laptop, scrolling through the list of incidents. "The plan is to understand. Who is this person? Why are they doing this? And why now?"

"Because the system is broken," Cole said. "That's why."

"Maybe. But there's more to it than that." Sienna clicked on one of the incident reports. "Look at the pattern. The first few rescues were reactive—animals in immediate danger, close proximity. But the more recent ones are different. They're targeted. Deliberate. Like someone who's not just responding to emergencies, but actively seeking them out."

"So the Ghost is escalating."

"Or evolving. From rescuer to vigilante."

Cole set his coffee down. "That's a problem."

"It is. But it's also a clue." Sienna pulled up the map. "If the Ghost is targeting specific cases, they have to be getting their information from somewhere. Social media, maybe. Or neighborhood forums. Or—"

"Or they're monitoring 911 calls," Cole finished.

Sienna nodded. "Which means they have access to information most people don't."

"Or they're just paying attention."

"Either way, it gives us a starting point." Sienna opened a new document. "We pull records of 911 calls related to animal distress in the target area. Cross-reference them with the Ghost's interventions. See if there's overlap."

"And if there is?"

"Then we know how they're finding their targets. And if we know that, we can predict where they'll go next."

Cole raised an eyebrow. "You want to set a trap."

"I want to understand," Sienna said. "The trap comes later."

By late afternoon, Sienna had pulled six months' worth of 911 call records related to animal welfare. The list was longer than she'd expected—over two hundred calls, ranging from barking complaints to reports of abuse and neglect. Most had been logged, triaged, and either resolved or closed due to lack of resources.

She cross-referenced the calls with the Ghost's eight interventions. Five of them matched.

Sienna stared at the screen, her pulse quickening. Five out of eight. That wasn't coincidence. That was a pattern.

The Ghost was monitoring the calls. Which meant they had access to information that wasn't public. Either they were connected to someone in the system—dispatch, animal control, maybe even the police—or they were finding the information another way.

She picked up her phone and called Tommy.

"Chen," he answered.

"It's Halbrook. I need you to pull something for me."

"Shoot."

"I need a list of everyone with access to 911 call records related to animal welfare. Dispatch, animal control, shelter staff, anyone who might have visibility into those reports."

Tommy was quiet for a moment. "You think the Ghost has inside help?"

"I think the Ghost has information they shouldn't have. And I want to know how they're getting it."

"Got it. I'll have it for you by tomorrow morning."

"Thanks, Tommy."

She hung up and turned back to her laptop. The pieces were starting to come together. Not the full picture—not yet—but the edges of it. The Ghost wasn't just a vigilante. They were organized. Informed. Strategic.

And that made them both more impressive and more dangerous.

Cole walked in, carrying two sandwiches from the deli down the street. He set one on Sienna's desk. "You've been at that screen for three hours. Eat something."

Sienna unwrapped the sandwich, took a bite, and kept typing. "I found a pattern."

"Of course you did."

"Five of the Ghost's interventions match 911 calls that were logged but not resolved. The Ghost is monitoring the system and stepping in when we don't."

Cole sat down, chewing thoughtfully. "So they're not just reacting. They're tracking."

"Exactly."

"Which means they're either connected to someone on the inside, or they're hacking the system."

"Or they're just really good at finding public information," Sienna said. "A lot of 911 calls get posted on social media. Neighborhood forums. NextDoor. Reddit. If you know where to look, you can piece together a pretty clear picture."

"So the Ghost is a data nerd with a conscience."

Sienna almost smiled. "Something like that."

Cole finished his sandwich. "You know, the more we learn about this person, the less I want to catch them."

"I know."

"But we're going to anyway."

"We are."

"Because that's the job."

"Because that's the job," Sienna agreed.

They sat in silence, the weight of it settling between them.

"For what it's worth," Cole said, "I think Tommy's right. This person isn't dangerous. They're just trying to help."

"Helping doesn't make it legal."

"No. But it makes it complicated."

That night, Sienna stayed late at the office, going through the call records one more time. She pulled up the details of each incident, reading through the notes.

One call stood out. A report from three weeks ago about a dog chained in a backyard with no shelter. The caller had been a neighbor, concerned but unwilling to get involved. The call had been logged, assigned to animal control, and then closed due to lack of resources.

Two days later, the Ghost had intervened.

Sienna pulled up the address, cross-referenced it with the map, and marked it with a red pin. Then she pulled up the next call. Same pattern. Report logged. No response. Ghost intervened.

She leaned back in her chair.

The Ghost wasn't just filling gaps. They were cleaning up the system's failures. One rescue at a time.

And Sienna didn't know whether to admire them or arrest them.

Her phone buzzed. A text from Cole.

Go home, Halbrook. The Ghost will still be out there tomorrow.

Sienna smiled, closed her laptop, and grabbed her jacket.

Cole was right. The Ghost would still be out there tomorrow.

And so would she.

Chapter 8
Rescue #3 - The Locked Warehouse

The pulse hit at 11:47 p.m., sharp and insistent, threaded with multiple voices. Not one animal. Several. Close together. Panicked.

Kai was halfway through sketching a lock mechanism when the sensation cut through his concentration like a blade. He set down his pen, closed his eyes, and tried to isolate the source. Dogs. Three, maybe four. Trapped. Overheating. The fear was layered, chaotic, a chorus of distress.

This was different from the usual signals. Most of the time, the distress came in waves—building, peaking, fading. This was constant. Sustained. Like the animals had been trapped for hours, their panic calcifying into exhaustion.

He grabbed his jacket, checked his kit—picks, tension wrenches, penlight, water bottle—and headed out. His hands were already moving through the mental choreography of the rescue before he'd even left the building. Assess the situation. Identify the lock type. Work the mechanism. Extract the animals. Leave no trace.

Except lately, he'd been leaving traces. Too many of them.

The signal led him east, toward the industrial zone near the waterfront. The streets here were wider, emptier, lined with warehouses and distribution centers that operated on skeleton crews after dark. Sodium lights cast everything in shades of amber and shadow. The air smelled like diesel and salt water.

Kai moved quickly, hood up, hands in pockets, following the pulse as it sharpened and clarified. The dogs were close. Very close.

He found them ten minutes later, in the back lot of a delivery warehouse. A white box truck sat parked near the loading dock, engine off, lights dark. The pulse was coming from inside.

Kai stopped at the edge of the lot, staying in the shadows, and assessed the situation. This was bigger than anything he'd done before. More exposed. More risk.

The warehouse was a two-story concrete structure with loading bays along one side and a small office entrance on the other. Security lights bathed the lot in harsh white light. A chain-link fence separated the lot from the street, topped with barbed wire. Two cameras—one covering the loading dock, one covering the truck. No guards visible.

Kai crouched behind a dumpster and studied the layout. The truck was locked, probably alarmed. The cameras had overlapping fields of view. The only blind spot was directly behind the truck, but that meant climbing the fence and crossing twenty feet of open pavement.

He could abort. Walk away. Find an easier target.

But the pulse was getting stronger. The dogs were suffering. And he was the only one who could hear them.

He needed a distraction.

Kai scanned the lot. A stack of pallets near the fence. A row of trash bins along the wall. A maintenance shed with a flickering light. Nothing immediately useful.

Then he heard it—a low rumble from inside the truck. Barking. Muffled, desperate.

The pulse intensified. Kai's hands tightened into fists.

He didn't have time to be careful. He had to move.

He pulled out his phone, opened a timer app, and set it for thirty seconds. Then he walked to the far end of the lot, placed the phone on the ground near the trash bins, and hit start. The phone's alarm was loud—obnoxiously loud.

Kai moved quickly, circling back toward the truck, staying low. The alarm went off right on cue. He counted to five, then heard the sound of a door opening. A security guard stepped out, flashlight in hand, walking toward the noise.

Kai didn't wait. He sprinted to the truck, pulled out his pick set, and went to work on the lock.

The mechanism was a standard pin tumbler, but the truck was newer, the lock tighter than the ones he'd practiced on. He worked the tension wrench, applied pressure, and started setting the pins. One. Two. The third pin stuck. He adjusted the angle, tried again. The pin set.

The barking inside the truck grew louder. The dogs had heard him.

Kai glanced over his shoulder. The guard was still at the far end of the lot, shining his flashlight into the trash bins. Kai had maybe thirty seconds.

He set the fourth pin. The fifth. The lock turned.

The truck's alarm blared.

Kai froze. The sound was deafening, a high-pitched wail that cut through the night. The guard spun around, flashlight swinging toward the truck.

"Hey!" the guard shouted. "Stop right there!"

Kai yanked the truck door open. Three dogs tumbled out—mutts, medium-sized, panting and terrified. They scattered immediately, running in different directions. One of them paused, looked back at Kai for a split second—eyes wide, ears flat—then bolted.

The guard was running now, flashlight beam bouncing across the pavement. "Stop! Police!"

Kai slammed the truck door shut, pocketed his tools, and ran. His boots hit the pavement hard. The guard was closing the distance, younger and faster than Kai had expected.

He vaulted the chain-link fence, caught his jacket on the barbed wire, felt it tear. He landed hard on the other side, stumbled, caught himself, and kept moving. Behind him, the alarm continued to wail. The guard was shouting into a radio, calling for backup.

Kai turned the corner, ducked into an alley, and pressed himself against the wall, breathing hard. His heart was pounding. His hands were shaking. The pulse in his head had eased—the dogs were free— but the adrenaline was still coursing through him.

Too close.

He waited, listening for sirens. Thirty seconds. A minute. Nothing. The guard must have stayed at the warehouse, securing the scene.

Kai pushed off the wall and started walking, forcing himself to slow down, to blend in. Just another person out late.

But his jacket was torn. His phone was gone. And somewhere, a camera had caught him.

He thought about going back for the phone—it was still sitting by the trash bins. But going back was suicide. The guard would be watching. The police might already be on their way.

Kai turned and walked deeper into the industrial zone. He kept his head down, his pace steady, his hands in his pockets.

The Ghost was leaving a trail. And sooner or later, someone was going to follow it.

By the time Kai got home, it was past one a.m. He dropped his jacket on the chair, kicked off his boots, and went straight to the bathroom sink. His reflection stared back at him—wired, exhausted, caught between relief and fear.

He'd gotten sloppy. The alarm. The guard. The cameras. Any one of those things could have ended with him in handcuffs.

But the dogs were free. That was what mattered.

He splashed cold water on his face, counted his breaths.

It didn't work.

He walked into the main room, dropped onto the futon, and pulled out his notebook. He opened it to a blank page and started writing.

Mistakes:

1. Didn't account for truck alarm. Should have researched the model.

2. Distraction was effective but left evidence (phone).

3. Guard response faster than expected. Need better timing.

4. Cameras. Didn't disable them. Probably caught something.

He stared at the list, jaw tight. The mistakes were adding up. And mistakes got you caught.

He closed the notebook, set it on the table.

The smart thing to do would be to stop. Lay low for a few weeks. Let the heat die down. But the signals wouldn't stop. They never did.

And neither would he.

The next morning, Kai walked into Brennan's and clocked in. Marcus was already at his workstation, sanding down a table leg, headphones in. Kai grabbed his apron, pulled out his phone—his backup phone, the one he kept for emergencies—and checked the news.

The headline hit him immediately.

Mysterious Break-In at Delivery Warehouse; Three Dogs Freed

He clicked the link, heart pounding.

Security footage from a local delivery warehouse shows an unidentified individual breaking into a locked truck late last night, freeing three dogs that had been accidentally trapped inside. The individual triggered the truck's alarm and fled the scene before security could apprehend them.

Police are investigating the incident, which appears to be connected to a string of similar animal rescues over the past six months. The individual, dubbed "the Ghost" by local media, has become a controversial figure —praised by animal welfare advocates and criticized by law enforcement.

"This person is breaking the law," said Captain Ortiz of the city's police department. "Regardless of their intentions, they're committing crimes, and we will hold them accountable."

The three dogs were later recovered by animal control and are currently being held at a local shelter.

Kai closed the article, set his phone down.

They had footage. They were investigating. The net was tightening.

He should stop. He knew that. Every rational part of his brain was screaming at him to stop.

But the signals were still there. Waiting.

And so was he.

That night, Kai didn't follow the signals. Instead, he sat on the rooftop, trying to figure out what came next.

The Ghost had become something bigger than him. A symbol. A story. And now, the police were actively hunting him. It was only a matter of time before they connected the dots.

He thought about the footage. What had the cameras caught? His build, probably. His gait. Maybe a partial view of his face, depending on the angle. He'd been careful, but careful wasn't the same as invisible.

And tonight, he hadn't been careful. He'd been desperate.

The alarm. The guard. The torn jacket. The abandoned phone. Each one a mistake. Each one a breadcrumb leading back to him.

He could feel the net tightening. The police had resources he didn't. Technology. Manpower. Legal authority. All he had was the signals and the ability to pick a lock.

It wasn't enough.

But it was all he had.

He pulled out his phone and opened the notes app. The list of rescues had grown to twenty-one now. Twenty-one animals saved. Twenty-one interventions that the system had failed to provide.

But how many more could he do before he got caught?

He stared at the list, then closed the app.

The pulse was there, faint but persistent. Somewhere south. Not urgent, but present.

Kai stood, walked to the edge of the roof, and looked down at the city below.

He could stop. Walk away. Let the Ghost fade into memory.

Or he could keep going. Smarter. More careful. Better.

He thought about the dogs in the truck. The way they'd tumbled out, panting and terrified, running toward freedom. The way the pulse had eased when they were safe.

That was why he did this. Not for the myth. Not for the recognition. But for the moments when the suffering stopped and something lived that would have died.

Kai pulled his hood up, turned away from the edge, and headed for the stairs.

Not for drama, for anonymity.

And this time, he'd be ready.

The security footage from the warehouse was grainy, but it was enough. Sienna watched it three times, sitting in the forensics lab with Tommy and Cole, studying every frame.

The figure appeared at 11:52 p.m., moving quickly across the lot. They crouched beside the truck, worked the lock, and opened the door. The alarm went off. The dogs ran. The figure fled.

But in one frame—just one—the angle was right. The security light caught the side of the figure's face as they turned to run.

Not enough for a clear ID. But enough to see features. Jawline. Cheekbone. The edge of a hood.

Sienna leaned forward. "Can you enhance that?"

Tommy was already working, his fingers flying across the keyboard. The image sharpened, pixel by pixel. The face became clearer. Still not enough for facial recognition, but enough to build a profile.

Male. Mid-twenties. Caucasian. Clean-shaven. No visible scars or distinguishing marks.

"That's him," Cole said. "That's the Ghost."

Sienna didn't respond. She stared at the screen, at the figure frozen in mid-flight, caught between shadow and light. There was something in the posture—not panic, but determination. Not recklessness, but purpose.

This wasn't someone who enjoyed breaking the law. This was someone who couldn't stop themselves.

Tommy zoomed in, enhanced the image as much as the resolution would allow. "This is the best we've got. Male, probably mid-twenties. Caucasian. Average build."

Sienna stared at the image. It wasn't much. But it was more than they'd had before.

"Can you run it through facial recognition?" she asked.

"Already did. No matches. Either he's not in the system, or the angle's too partial."

Cole leaned over Sienna's shoulder. "So we've got a partial face, a locksmith's tool case, and a pattern of rescues. What's next?"

Sienna didn't answer. She was still staring at the screen, at the figure frozen mid-flight.

The Ghost was real. And they were getting closer.

"Next," she said finally, "we figure out where he's going to strike next. And we're there waiting."

Chapter 9
The Task Force Gears Up

The war room wasn't actually a war room. It was a converted conference space on the third floor, too small for the number of people crammed into it, with a whiteboard that had seen better days and a projector that flickered every time someone walked past it.

Sienna stood at the front, marker in hand, staring at the whiteboard. She'd divided it into sections: **Timeline**, **Locations**, **Methods**, **Profile**, and **Next Steps**. Each section was half-filled with notes, data points, and questions that didn't have answers yet.

Behind her, the team was assembling. Cole sat in the front row, coffee in hand. Tommy Chen had claimed a corner desk, laptop open. Two patrol officers—Jenkins and Ramirez—sat near the back, notebooks out. And standing near the door, arms crossed, was Captain Ortiz.

Sienna turned to face them. "All right. Let's get started."

Ortiz stepped forward. "Before we dive in, I want to set expectations. This case has become a political hot potato. The mayor's office is getting calls from both sides—people who think the Ghost is a hero, and people who think we're not doing enough to stop them. City hall wants results. Fast."

"Define 'fast,'" Cole said.

"Two weeks. Maybe three if we're lucky. After that, they're going to start asking why we're spending resources on a case where no one's been hurt."

Sienna felt her jaw tighten. "The victims are animals. That doesn't make them less important."

"I agree. But I'm not the one you need to convince. The mayor's office sees this as a PR problem, not a criminal one. Our job is to solve it before it becomes both."

The room went quiet. Sienna could feel the pressure to move fast, to close the case, to deliver a result that satisfied everyone. Which was impossible.

"Understood," Sienna said. She turned back to the whiteboard. "Let's talk about what we know."

She tapped the **Timeline** section. "Twenty-one confirmed interventions over the past six months. The frequency has increased —one in the first month, three in the second, five in the third. The most recent incident was three nights ago at the delivery warehouse."

"So the Ghost is escalating," Jenkins said.

"Or getting more confident. The early rescues were opportunistic —animals in immediate danger, close proximity, minimal risk. The more recent ones are targeted. Deliberate. The Ghost is actively seeking out cases of neglect and abuse."

She moved to the **Locations** section, where she'd pinned a map with red dots marking each intervention. "All twenty-one incidents fall within a five-mile radius. Most cluster in two neighborhoods—the west side residential area and the industrial zone near the waterfront."

Tommy pulled up a digital version of the map, projecting it onto the screen. "I ran a geographic profile. If we assume the Ghost is operating from a central location—home or workplace—the most likely area is here." He highlighted a section. "Roughly a two-square-mile zone."

"What's in that area?" Ortiz asked.

"Residential housing, small businesses, a few industrial facilities. Nothing that stands out. But if we cross-reference with locksmith businesses, repair shops, or anyone with access to professional-grade tools, we might get a hit."

Sienna made a note. "Good. Let's pull a list of locksmiths and related businesses in that zone. We'll start with interviews."

"What about the footage from the warehouse?" Ramirez asked. "Did we get an ID?"

Sienna shook her head. "Partial face, but not enough for facial recognition. Male, mid-twenties, Caucasian, clean-shaven. Average build. No distinguishing marks."

"So we've got a generic white guy in a hoodie," Cole said. "That narrows it down to about half the city."

"It's more than we had yesterday. And it confirms what we suspected—the Ghost is young, physically capable, and trained."

She moved to the **Methods** section. "Lockpicking. Surveillance evasion. Animal handling. The Ghost knows how to bypass security, avoid cameras, and work quickly under pressure. That suggests prior training or professional experience."

Tommy nodded. "I've been looking at the tools visible in the footage. Professional-grade picks, compact case, efficient technique. This person either works in the field or has extensive practice."

"So we're looking for a locksmith," Jenkins said.

"Or someone adjacent to the field. Security, maintenance, property management. Anyone with access to locks and the skills to bypass them."

She turned to the **Profile** section. "Here's what we know about the Ghost as a person. Motivated by empathy for animals. No evidence of financial gain or personal benefit. Operates alone. Avoids confrontation. Leaves notes with 'DO MORE,' suggesting a desire to provoke change or challenge the system."

"Sounds like someone with a savior complex," Ortiz said.

"Or someone who's seen the system fail too many times. The Ghost isn't stealing. They're not hurting anyone. They're filling gaps that we're not filling."

"That doesn't make it legal," ADA Clarence Lee said from the doorway. He'd slipped in during the briefing, tablet in hand, expression unreadable. "Vigilantism is still a crime, Detective. Regardless of the motivation."

"I'm aware," Sienna said.

"Are you? Because from where I'm standing, it sounds like you're sympathizing with the suspect."

"I'm trying to understand the suspect. There's a difference."

"Not to a jury."

The room went tense. Sienna held Lee's gaze. "If we want to catch the Ghost, we need to understand why they're doing this. And the answer isn't as simple as 'savior complex.' The answer is that the system is broken, and someone decided to fix it."

"By breaking the law," Lee said.

"By saving lives," Sienna shot back.

Ortiz stepped between them. "All right. Let's stay focused. Lee, what's your concern?"

Lee set his tablet on the table. "My concern is that this case is generating public sympathy for a criminal. If we don't handle it carefully, we risk turning the Ghost into a martyr. And if that happens, we'll have copycats."

"So what do you suggest?" Sienna asked.

"I suggest we move quickly and quietly. Identify the suspect, bring them in, and prosecute. No media circus. No public debate. Just a clean resolution."

"And if the public doesn't see it that way?" Cole asked.

"Then we deal with it. But we don't let the narrative get away from us."

Sienna turned back to the whiteboard. Lee wasn't wrong. The

Ghost had become a symbol, and symbols were dangerous. But shutting down the conversation wasn't the answer.

"Next steps," she said, tapping the final section. "We pull a list of locksmiths and related businesses in the target zone. We interview them. We monitor social media and neighborhood forums for reports of animal distress—if the Ghost is tracking those, we might be able to predict their next move. And we coordinate with animal control to flag high-risk cases."

"You want to set a trap," Ortiz said.

"I want to be ready. If the Ghost is targeting specific cases, we need to know which ones. And if we can get there first, we can intercept them."

Ortiz considered this, then nodded. "All right. You've got two weeks. Use them wisely."

He left the room, Lee following. The door closed, and the tension eased.

Cole leaned back in his chair. "Well, that was fun."

"Define 'fun,'" Tommy said.

"I was being sarcastic."

Sienna set the marker down and turned to the team. "All right. Let's get to work. Jenkins, Ramirez—start pulling the list of locksmiths. Tommy, keep working on the geographic profile. Cole, you're with me. We're going to talk to animal control."

The team dispersed, leaving Sienna alone with Cole. He walked over to the whiteboard.

"You really think we can catch them?" he asked.

"I think we can try."

"And if we do? What then?"

Sienna stared at the map, at the red dots marking the Ghost's interventions. Each one a life saved. Each one a crime committed.

"I don't know," she said.

Cole nodded. "Yeah. Me neither."

. . .

That afternoon, Sienna and Cole drove to the city's main animal control facility. It was a low-slung building on the edge of the industrial zone, surrounded by chain-link fencing and the constant sound of barking.

They were met at the entrance by Tessa Morales, a senior animal control officer Sienna had worked with before. Tessa was in her early thirties, with short dark hair, tired eyes, and the kind of no-nonsense demeanor that came from years of dealing with the worst humanity had to offer.

"Detective Halbrook," Tessa said, shaking Sienna's hand. "I heard you were working the Ghost case."

"Word travels fast."

"It's all anyone's talking about. Half the staff thinks the Ghost is a hero. The other half thinks they're making our jobs harder."

"Which half are you in?" Cole asked.

Tessa smiled grimly. "The half that wishes the system worked well enough that we didn't need a Ghost."

She led them inside, through a maze of hallways lined with kennels. The sound of barking was overwhelming. They passed rows of cages—dogs, cats, a few rabbits—all waiting for homes that might never come.

"We're at 150 percent capacity," Tessa said, raising her voice over the noise. "We've got animals sleeping in hallways, in offices, anywhere we can fit them. And we're still getting calls every day. We can't keep up."

"How many calls do you get in a week?" Sienna asked.

"Fifty, maybe sixty. We respond to about half. The rest get triaged or closed due to lack of resources."

"And the ones that get closed?"

Tessa stopped walking, turned to face Sienna. "Some of them die. Some of them suffer until someone else intervenes. And some of them get rescued by the Ghost."

Sienna pulled out her tablet. "I need to see the calls that were logged but not resolved. Specifically, the ones in the west side and industrial zone over the past six months."

Tessa nodded. "I can pull that for you. But I'll tell you right now, it's a long list."

"How long?"

"Over a hundred cases."

Sienna felt her stomach drop. "A hundred?"

"We're understaffed, underfunded, and overwhelmed. The Ghost isn't the problem, Detective. The Ghost is a symptom."

By the time Sienna and Cole got back to the precinct, it was late afternoon. Sienna dropped into her chair, opened her laptop, and started cross-referencing the animal control data with the Ghost's interventions. The overlap was undeniable. Five of the Ghost's rescues matched calls that had been logged but not resolved. Another three matched cases that had been closed due to lack of resources.

The Ghost wasn't just filling gaps. They were cleaning up the system's messes.

Cole walked in, carrying two sandwiches. He set one on Sienna's desk. "Eat something. You've been at that screen for three hours."

Sienna took the sandwich, unwrapped it, and took a bite. "We're not going to catch them."

"What?"

"We're not going to catch them. Not unless they make a mistake. And even if we do, I don't know if we should."

Cole sat down, his expression serious. "Halbrook—"

"I know. I know we have a job to do. I know the law is the law. But the more I dig into this, the more I realize that the Ghost is right. The system is broken. And someone had to do something."

"That doesn't make it legal."

"No. But it makes it necessary."

They sat in silence, the weight of it settling between them.

"So what do we do?" Cole asked.

Sienna stared at the map on her screen, at the red dots marking the Ghost's interventions.

"We do our job," she said. "And we hope that when we find them, we understand why."

Cole nodded. "Yeah. Me too."

Chapter 10
Media Mythmaking

Mina's phone buzzed at 7:23 a.m., pulling her out of a dream she couldn't remember. She fumbled for it on the nightstand, squinting at the screen. An unknown number. She almost let it go to voicemail, but something made her answer.

"Mina Torres," she said, her voice rough with sleep.

"Ms. Torres, my name is Eddie Ruiz. I work security at Westside Distribution. I think I have something you'd want to see."

Mina sat up, suddenly awake. "What kind of something?"

"Footage. From last night. Someone broke into one of our trucks and freed three dogs that were locked inside. The cops are coming to take a statement, but I thought you'd want to know first. You know, since you wrote that article about the Ghost."

Mina's pulse quickened. "Can you send me the footage?"

"I can do better. I can meet you. But it has to be now, before my shift ends."

Twenty minutes later, Mina was in her car, driving toward the industrial zone with a travel mug of coffee and a recorder in her bag.

The Ghost had struck again. And this time, she was going to be the first to report it.

Eddie Ruiz met her in the parking lot of a 24-hour diner. He was in his early forties, stocky, with a tired face and a security uniform that had seen better days. He slid into the booth across from her, set his phone on the table.

"Thanks for meeting me," Mina said, pulling out her recorder. "Do you mind if I record this?"

Eddie glanced at the recorder, then nodded. "Yeah, that's fine. But I don't want my name in the article. I could lose my job."

"Understood. I'll keep you anonymous."

Eddie relaxed slightly. He pulled up a video on his phone and turned it toward Mina. "This is from last night, around midnight. Watch."

Mina leaned in, watching the grainy footage. A figure in a hoodie approached a white box truck, crouched beside it, and worked the lock. The truck's alarm went off. Dogs tumbled out. The figure ran.

Mina's breath caught. It was the Ghost. No question.

"Did you see them in person?" she asked.

"I heard the alarm and ran out, but they were already gone. Fast. Like they knew exactly what they were doing."

"And the dogs?"

"Animal control picked them up this morning. They're fine. But if that person hadn't intervened, they would've died. It was hot in that truck. No ventilation."

Mina made notes, her mind racing. "Do you know how the dogs got locked in there?"

Eddie's expression darkened. "Driver negligence. The guy left them in there while he went to a bar. Came back hours later, drunk, didn't even realize they were still inside. The company's doing an internal investigation, but between you and me, this isn't the first time something like this has happened."

"And no one reported it?"

"Who's going to report it? The driver? The company? They don't want the liability." Eddie leaned back, crossing his arms. "Look, I'm not saying what the Ghost did was legal. But I am saying that if they hadn't done it, those dogs would be dead. So you tell me—who's the criminal here?"

Mina didn't answer. She was staring at the video, at the figure frozen mid-flight.

"Can you send me this footage?" she asked.

Eddie hesitated. "The cops are going to want it."

"I'm sure they'll get a copy. But I'd like one too. For the story."

Eddie considered this, then nodded. "Yeah, okay. But you didn't get it from me."

"Understood."

He sent the file to her email, finished his coffee, and stood. "One more thing. I don't know who the Ghost is. But whoever they are, they're doing something the rest of us aren't. And maybe that's worth something."

He left before Mina could respond.

By the time Mina got back to her apartment, it was almost nine a.m. She made another pot of coffee, opened her laptop, and started writing.

The words came fast. She'd been thinking about this story since the first article, trying to figure out what it meant. The Ghost wasn't just a vigilante. They were a symbol. A challenge. A mirror reflecting the system's failures.

She wrote for two hours straight. When she finally leaned back and read through the draft, she felt a mix of pride and unease.

The Ghost Strikes Again: A City's Reckoning
By Mina Torres
Three dogs are alive today because someone broke the law.
Late last night, an unidentified individual—dubbed "the Ghost"

by local media—broke into a delivery truck at a westside warehouse and freed three dogs that had been locked inside for hours. The dogs, left by a negligent driver, were suffering from heat exhaustion and dehydration. If the Ghost hadn't intervened, they would have died.

This is the twenty-first confirmed rescue attributed to the Ghost over the past six months. Each one follows the same pattern: a locked animal in distress, a system too slow or too overwhelmed to respond, and a vigilante who steps in to fill the gap.

The Ghost doesn't ask for recognition. Doesn't wait for thanks. Doesn't operate within the bounds of the law. But in a city where animal welfare resources are stretched thin, the Ghost is doing what the system can't—or won't.

Police are actively investigating, and city officials have called for swift action. Captain Ortiz emphasized that "vigilantism, regardless of intent, is a crime."

But the question remains: if the system is failing, and someone steps in to save lives, who is the real criminal?

The Ghost's interventions have sparked a citywide debate about animal welfare, systemic failure, and the role of individual action. Some see the Ghost as a hero. Others see them as a dangerous precedent. But one thing is clear: the Ghost is forcing us to confront uncomfortable truths about the systems we rely on—and the gaps they leave behind.

Mina read through the article twice, then sat back. It was good. Maybe the best thing she'd written. But it was also dangerous.

She was feeding the myth. Making the Ghost bigger. And if the Ghost got caught, this article would be part of the reason why.

Her phone buzzed. A text from her editor.

Got your draft. Love it. Can you get it to me by noon? Want to run it tonight.

Mina stared at the message, her thumb hovering over the keyboard.

She could pull the story. Say she needed more time.

Or she could hit send.

She thought about Eddie Ruiz, asking who the real criminal was. She thought about the dogs in the truck, hours away from death. She thought about the Ghost, risking arrest to do what no one else would.

And she thought about the system that had made the Ghost necessary.

She hit send.

The article went live at 6 p.m. By 8 p.m., it had been shared over a thousand times. By midnight, it was trending on social media, generating heated debates across the internet.

Mina sat at her desk, scrolling through the responses, her stomach twisting.

This was what she'd wanted. A story that broke through the noise. But now that she had it, she wasn't sure how to feel.

The comments were split. The animal welfare advocates who saw the Ghost as a hero. The law-and-order types who saw them as a criminal. And then there were the outliers—the people who wanted to be the Ghost, who saw the article as permission to take justice into their own hands.

That was the part that scared her.

@AnimalAdvocate87: *Finally, someone with the guts to say it. The Ghost is a hero. Period.*

@LawAndOrder2025: *This is dangerous. Vigilantism is not the answer.*

@ShelterVolunteer: *I work in animal welfare—the system is broken. The Ghost is doing what we can't.*

@Inspired2Act: *The Ghost is showing us what's possible. If they can do it, so can we. Time to take action.*

Mina closed the browser, leaned back.

She'd done her job. She'd told the story. But she'd also made the Ghost into something bigger than a person. A symbol. A myth. And myths were hard to control.

She thought about journalism school, about the ethics classes that had seemed so abstract. The responsibility of the press. The power of narrative. The line between reporting and advocacy.

She'd crossed that line. She knew that. The article wasn't just reporting facts—it was framing them. Asking questions that led readers toward a specific conclusion.

But what was the alternative? Ignore the story? Write a neutral piece that said nothing and changed nothing?

She'd made her choice. And now she had to live with it.

Her phone buzzed. Another text from her editor.

Great work. Want you to do a follow-up. Interviews with activists, shelter workers. Let's keep this momentum going.

Mina stared at the message. Keep the momentum going. That's what editors always said. Ride the wave. Milk the story. Get the clicks.

But this wasn't just about clicks. This was about a person—a real person—who was risking their freedom. And every article she wrote made them more visible. More vulnerable.

She thought about the Ghost, somewhere out there, reading her article. Did they feel validated? Exposed? Scared?

She didn't know. And that was the problem.

Because journalists weren't supposed to be part of the story. They were supposed to observe it, report it, let the public decide what it meant.

But Mina wasn't observing anymore. She was shaping. Building. Creating a narrative that had taken on a life of its own.

And she didn't know how to stop it.

Across the city, Kai sat on his futon, staring at his phone. Mina's article was open on the screen, the words blurring together as he read them for the third time.

Three dogs are alive today because someone broke the law.

He set the phone down, closed his eyes.

The Ghost wasn't just him anymore. It was a story. A myth. A symbol that people either loved or hated.

And Mina Torres had made it bigger.

He didn't know whether to thank her or curse her.

Part of him felt validated. The article understood what he was doing. It asked the right questions. Made people think about the system instead of just the person breaking the law.

But another part of him felt exposed. Every article made him more visible. More recognizable. More likely to get caught.

He scrolled through the comments. Some called him a hero. Others called him a criminal. A few called him both.

One comment stood out:

@Inspired2Act: *The Ghost is showing us what's possible. If they can do it, so can we.*

Kai's stomach dropped.

Copycats.

He closed the app, set the phone down.

The Ghost had started as a response to suffering. But now it was becoming something else. A movement. A symbol.

And Kai didn't know if that was a good thing or a terrible one.

In the task force war room, Sienna stared at the same article on her laptop, her jaw tight. Cole stood behind her, reading over her shoulder.

"Well," Cole said. "That's going to make things interesting."

Sienna didn't respond. She was staring at the line: *The Ghost is forcing us to confront uncomfortable truths about the systems we rely on—and the gaps they leave behind.*

Mina Torres wasn't wrong. But she was also making Sienna's job harder.

"She's building a myth," Sienna said.

"Yeah. And myths are hard to catch."

Sienna scrolled through the comments. The support. The criticism. The calls to action.

"Ortiz is going to lose his mind when he sees this," Cole said.

"Probably."

Cole sat down beside her. "So what's the play?"

Sienna thought for a moment. "The play is that we use this. Mina's article just gave us a roadmap. She's highlighting the pattern, the systemic failures, the areas where the Ghost is most active. If we cross-reference her reporting with our data, we can narrow the search."

"You want to use the journalist to catch the vigilante."

"I want to use every resource we have. Including the media."

Cole nodded slowly. "Smart. But risky. If Mina figures out we're using her work, she's going to write about it."

"Let her. By then, we'll have the Ghost."

She closed the laptop, stood, and walked to the whiteboard. She stared at the map, at the red dots marking the Ghost's interventions.

Somewhere out there, the Ghost was reading the same article. Feeling the same pressure.

The myth was growing. The net was tightening.

And Sienna was going to find them.

Even if she didn't know what she'd do when she did.

Chapter 11
Lock & Key

The pulse hit at 9:47 p.m., sharp and urgent, cutting through the noise of the city like a blade. Kai was walking home from the hardware store, a new set of tension wrenches in his pocket, when the sensation stopped him mid-stride.

A dog. Trapped. Overheating. Close by.

He closed his eyes, tried to isolate the source. Downtown. Maybe six blocks east. The signal was strong, insistent, threaded with panic.

Kai changed direction and started walking.

The parking garage was a six-story concrete structure wedged between two office buildings. It was the kind of place that looked abandoned even when it wasn't—dim lighting, oil stains on the pavement, the faint smell of exhaust and decay. Kai had passed it a dozen times but never paid much attention. Now, standing at the entrance, he could feel the pulse radiating from somewhere inside. No relief. No quiet.

Fourth floor. Maybe fifth.

He pulled his hood up, checked his kit—picks, tension wrenches, penlight, water bottle—and stepped inside.

The air was cooler inside, thick with the smell of concrete and motor oil. The lighting was sporadic, sodium bulbs flickering at irregular intervals. Kai's footsteps echoed off the walls, each sound amplified by the acoustics of the space.

He felt exposed. Vulnerable. But the pulse was too strong to ignore.

The garage was mostly empty. A few cars scattered across the lower levels. Kai took the stairs, moving quickly but quietly. The pulse grew stronger with each floor, sharpening into something almost unbearable.

By the time he reached the fourth floor, he could barely think.

He found the SUV near the far corner, parked under a flickering sodium light. The windows were cracked, but not enough. The dog inside—a golden retriever, panting hard—was pressed against the glass, eyes wide, tongue lolling. Foam at the corners of its mouth. The pulse was overwhelming now, a scream in Kai's head. It thrummed under everything, the way a migraine announces itself before pain.

Kai approached quickly, scanning the area. No cameras visible. No people. Just the hum of the city below and the echo of his own breathing.

He pulled out his pick set, selected the tools he needed, and went to work on the lock.

The mechanism was a standard pin tumbler, but the SUV was newer, the lock tighter than the ones he'd practiced on. The pins were set deeper, the springs stiffer. He worked the tension wrench, applied pressure, and started setting the pins. One. Two. The third pin stuck. He adjusted the angle, tried again. The pin resisted, then gave way.

The dog whined, a low, desperate sound. It scratched at the window, leaving streaks on the glass.

"I know," he muttered. "I'm working on it."

The third pin set. The fourth. His hands were steady, his movements precise, but his heart was pounding. Every second felt like an hour.

Fifth pin. The lock was fighting him, the mechanism worn but stubborn. He adjusted his grip, applied more pressure to the tension wrench. The pin set with a soft click.

Then he heard it—the sound of a car engine echoing up from the lower levels. Headlights swept across the walls. Kai froze, listening.

The engine cut off. Doors opened. Voices.

"—fourth floor, right?"

"That's what dispatch said."

Kai's pulse spiked. Police. They were here. And they were coming up.

He turned back to the lock, hands moving faster now. Fifth pin. Sixth. The lock turned.

The SUV's alarm blared.

Kai swore under his breath, yanked the door open, and reached inside. The dog scrambled out, panting, tail tucked, and bolted toward the stairwell. Kai slammed the door shut, silencing the alarm, and pocketed his tools.

The voices were closer now. Footsteps on the stairs.

Kai ran.

He sprinted toward the opposite stairwell, his boots hitting the concrete hard. The sound echoed off the walls, impossibly loud. The pulse in his head had eased—the dog was free—but the adrenaline was still coursing through him, sharp and electric.

Behind him, he heard the squeal of tires. The slam of car doors. The crackle of a radio.

He reached the stairwell, yanked the door open, and slipped inside just as the voices reached the fourth floor.

"—over here. That's the vehicle."

"Check the area. See if anyone's around."

Kai didn't wait. He took the stairs two at a time, descending as fast as he could without making noise. His heart was pounding so hard he could feel it in his throat. The stairwell was narrow, claustro-phobic, the concrete walls pressing in.

He could hear the voices above him, muffled by the concrete, but close enough to make his skin crawl. Footsteps. Radio chatter. The methodical sweep of flashlights.

Third floor. Second floor. Ground floor.

By the time he reached the exit, he was out of breath. He pushed through the door, stepped into the alley behind the garage, and forced himself to slow down. Head down. Hands in pockets. Just another person out late.

But his pulse was still racing. His hands were still shaking. And he could still hear the voices echoing in his head.

Too close. Way too close.

Sienna Halbrook stepped onto the fourth floor of the parking garage, flashlight in hand, scanning the area. Cole was beside her, radio in hand, coordinating with dispatch.

"Dispatch said someone reported a dog in distress," Cole said. "Fourth floor, near the northwest corner."

"Who called it in?"

"Anonymous tip. Came in about five minutes ago."

Sienna swept her flashlight across the rows of cars. Near the far corner, under a flickering sodium light, she saw it—a black SUV, windows cracked, driver's side door slightly ajar.

She approached cautiously, Cole trailing behind. The SUV was empty. No dog. No owner. Just the faint smell of wet fur and the echo of something that had happened moments before.

"Door's unlocked," Sienna said, pulling it open. The interior was clean, no signs of forced entry. But the lock mechanism looked scratched, the kind of wear that came from tools, not keys. Fresh scratches, the metal still bright where the pick had scraped against it.

Cole crouched beside her, shining his flashlight on the lock. "Someone picked this."

"Recently," Sienna said. She pulled out her phone, took a photo of the lock, then stood and scanned the area. The garage was quiet, but not empty. She could feel it—the residual energy of someone who'd been here moments before. "Where's the dog?"

"Probably ran. If someone freed it, it wouldn't stick around."

Sienna walked to the edge of the floor, looking down at the street below. A few pedestrians. A couple of cars. No sign of a dog. No sign of the Ghost.

But they'd been here. She could feel it. The timing was too perfect. The lock too fresh. The Ghost had been standing right where she was standing, working the lock, freeing the dog.

And then they'd vanished.

"Check the stairwells," she said. "Both of them. See if anyone's still in the building."

Cole nodded, spoke into his radio. Two patrol officers appeared from the stairs, split up, and started searching.

Sienna stayed by the SUV, staring at the scratched lock. The Ghost had been here. Minutes ago, maybe seconds. And they'd slipped away before she could catch them.

She pulled out her phone and called Tommy.

"Chen," he answered.

"It's Halbrook. I need you to pull footage from the parking garage at Fifth and Market. Fourth floor. Time stamp around 9:50 p.m."

"On it. What am I looking for?"

"The Ghost," Sienna said. "They were just here."

Kai made it three blocks before he stopped running. He ducked into a 24-hour diner, ordered coffee he didn't want, and sat in a booth near the back.

That was too close. Way too close.

He pulled out his phone, checked the news. Nothing yet. But it was only a matter of time before someone reported it. Another rescue. Another intervention. Another breadcrumb leading back to him.

He thought about the detective's voice, echoing up from the stairwell. Calm. Methodical. Professional. Not the voice of someone who was going to give up.

They were getting closer. He could feel it.

He finished his coffee, left cash on the table, and walked out into the night.

By the time Sienna got back to the precinct, it was past eleven. Tommy was waiting for her in the forensics lab, laptop open, footage queued up.

"Got something," he said, gesturing to the screen. "You're going to want to see this."

Sienna pulled up a chair, leaned in. The footage was black-and-white, shot from a camera mounted near the stairwell on the fourth floor. The timestamp read 9:52 p.m.

"Watch this," Tommy said, hitting play.

The video showed an empty parking level. A few cars. Flickering lights. Then, at 9:52:17, a figure appeared at the edge of the frame—hooded, moving fast, heading toward the stairwell. They reached the door, pulled it open, and disappeared inside. The whole sequence took less than three seconds.

Tommy paused the video, zoomed in on the figure. "That's the Ghost. No question."

Sienna stared at the screen. The figure was blurry, the angle wrong for a clear ID. But the posture was familiar. The way they moved. The efficiency. The same build as the warehouse footage. The same gait.

"Can you get a better angle?"

"Already tried. This is the only camera that caught them. But look at the movement." Tommy played the footage again, frame by frame. "See how they're running? Not panicked. Controlled. They know exactly where they're going."

Tommy rewound the footage, played it again. "Watch the timing. The figure appears at 9:52:17. You and Cole arrived on the fourth floor at 9:53:04. That's a forty-seven-second gap."

"Forty-seven seconds," Sienna repeated.

"Forty-seven seconds between the Ghost finishing the rescue and you arriving on scene. If you'd been thirty seconds faster, you would've caught them."

Sienna leaned back. Forty-seven seconds. Less than a minute. The Ghost had been right there, working the lock, freeing the dog, slipping away into the shadows.

And she'd missed them.

"We're getting closer," Tommy said.

"Not close enough," Sienna replied.

She stood, walked to the whiteboard in the corner of the lab, and added a new red pin to the map. The parking garage. The twenty-second intervention.

The Ghost was escalating. Getting bolder. Taking more risks.

And sooner or later, they were going to make a mistake.

Sienna just had to be there when they did.

Kai sat on the rooftop of his building, staring at the city.

Forty-seven seconds. That's how close it had been. Forty-seven seconds between freedom and arrest.

He thought about the detective's voice, echoing up from the stairwell. The sound of footsteps. The sweep of flashlights. They'd been right there, on the same floor, breathing the same air. If he'd been thirty seconds slower, if the lock had taken one more pin to set—he'd be in handcuffs right now.

The thought made his hands shake.

They were good. Professional. And they were getting closer with every rescue.

He pulled out his notebook, opened it to a blank page, and started writing.

Mistakes:

1. Didn't account for police response time. Should have monitored dispatch.

2. SUV alarm. Should have disabled it before opening the door.

3. Stayed too long. Should have been gone before they arrived.

4. Didn't check for secondary cameras. Got caught on footage.

He stared at the list, jaw tight. The mistakes were piling up. And mistakes got you caught.

He thought about stopping. Really stopping this time. Not just taking a break, but walking away completely. Letting the Ghost fade into memory.

But the alternative—doing nothing—felt like a betrayal of everything the signals had taught him. That suffering was real. That indifference was a choice. That someone had to act, even when it was dangerous, even when it was illegal, even when no one would thank you for it.

He closed the notebook, set it on the ground beside him.

The Ghost was running out of time. And Kai DuMoire didn't know how much longer he could keep running.

But he knew one thing: he wasn't going to stop.

Not yet.

Not while the signals kept calling.

And not while there were still animals out there, suffering in the gaps the system left behind.

Chapter 12
The Stairwell Echo

Sienna stood by the SUV, staring at the scratched lock. The patrol officers had searched both stairwells and found nothing. No sign of the Ghost. No sign of the dog. Just empty concrete and the echo of footsteps that had already faded.

But the Ghost had been here. Minutes ago. Close enough that Sienna could almost feel their presence.

Cole walked over, radio in hand. "Jenkins and Ramirez checked the perimeter. Nothing. Whoever it was, they're long gone."

Sienna didn't respond. She was examining the SUV's interior, her flashlight beam sweeping across the seats. The leather was clean, no signs of struggle. The windows had been cracked open. And there, on the passenger seat, was a small plastic water bottle, half-empty, sitting upright. The cap was off. Water had pooled on the leather.

It was deliberate. Careful. The Ghost hadn't just freed the dog—they'd made sure it had water.

"Look at this," she said, pointing.

Cole leaned in. "Water bottle. So?"

"So the Ghost left it. For the dog." Sienna pulled out her phone, took a photo. "They didn't just free the animal. They made sure it had water. They cared."

"Or they're just thorough."

"Same thing."

Sienna stepped back, scanning the area. The Ghost had been here, standing right where she was standing. And then they'd vanished. But people didn't just vanish. They left traces.

She walked to the stairwell door, the one farthest from where they'd arrived. The Ghost would have gone this way—away from the voices, into the shadows.

She pulled the door open and stepped inside.

The stairwell was narrow, claustrophobic, the concrete walls amplifying every sound. Sienna's flashlight beam cut through the darkness, illuminating the stairs descending below. The air was cooler here, damp, carrying the faint smell of mildew and exhaust. She started down, moving slowly, scanning each step.

Third floor. Nothing.

Second floor. Nothing.

Ground floor.

She stopped.

There, on the landing, was a wet footprint. Faint, but visible. The tread pattern was clear—a boot, size ten or eleven, worn at the heel. The water was still fresh, not yet fully evaporated.

And beside the footprint, crumpled against the wall, was a glove.

Sienna crouched, her pulse quickening. She pulled out an evidence bag, carefully picked up the glove. It was black, made of thin synthetic material, the kind you'd wear to avoid leaving fingerprints. But it was worn, the fingertips frayed, the palm stained with something dark—oil, maybe, or grease. The kind of wear that came from repeated use, from hands that worked with tools, with locks, with mechanisms that required precision.

This was real. Tangible. A piece of the Ghost, left behind in the rush to escape.

Cole appeared at the top of the stairs. "Find something?"

"Yeah," Sienna said, holding up the bag. "A glove. And a footprint."

Cole descended the stairs, crouched beside her. "Footprint's not much to go on. But the glove—that's DNA. Skin cells. Sweat. If we're lucky, we might get a match."

"If they're in the system."

"Big if."

Sienna stood, stared at the glove. The Ghost had been here. Moments ago. Close enough to touch. And they'd left something behind.

"Bag the footprint too," she said. "Get a cast made. I want everything analyzed."

Cole nodded, pulled out his radio, and called for the crime scene unit.

Sienna walked back up the stairs, her mind racing. The Ghost wasn't just a vigilante. They were skilled. Disciplined. Careful. But not perfect. And imperfection left traces.

She was going to find them.

By the time Sienna got back to the precinct, it was past midnight. The task force war room was empty, the whiteboard covered in notes and maps. She dropped into her chair, pulled out her laptop, and started typing.

Case Notes: Parking Garage Incident

Location: Fifth and Market, fourth floor

Time: Approx. 9:52 p.m.

Victim: Golden retriever, locked in SUV, heat exhaustion

Intervention: Lock picked, dog freed, water left at scene

Evidence Recovered: Water bottle, glove (DNA analysis pending), footprint (size 10-11 boot)

Observations:

- Ghost operates with precision and speed. Lock picked in under two minutes.
- No damage to vehicle. Clean extraction.
- Water left for animal suggests empathy, not just efficiency.
- Ghost aware of police presence but did not panic. Controlled escape.

Conclusion: Ghost is not a reckless amateur. This is someone with training, discipline, and a clear moral framework. They're doing it because they believe it's necessary.

Sienna leaned back. She'd been chasing the Ghost for weeks now, treating them like a puzzle to solve. But tonight, standing in that parking garage, holding that glove, she'd felt something shift.

The Ghost wasn't just a case. They were a person. Someone who cared enough to risk arrest. Someone who left water for a dying dog. Someone who operated in the shadows not because they wanted to, but because they had to.

And Sienna didn't know whether to admire them or arrest them.

Her phone buzzed. A text from Tommy.

Got the glove. Running DNA now. Should have results by tomorrow afternoon.

Sienna typed a reply.

Thanks. Let me know as soon as you have something.

She set the phone down, closed her laptop, and stared at the whiteboard. The map of the city. The red dots marking the Ghost's interventions. Twenty-two now. Twenty-two animals saved. Twenty-two crimes committed.

She thought about what Cole had said earlier. *You sound like you admire them.*

Maybe she did. A little.

But that didn't change the fact that the Ghost was breaking the law. And Sienna's job was to enforce it.

Even when the law felt inadequate.

. . .

The next morning, Sienna sat in Captain Ortiz's office, the glove in an evidence bag on the desk between them. Ortiz picked it up, studied it, then set it back down.

"DNA analysis is pending," Sienna said. "But even if we don't get a match, the glove tells us something. The Ghost is careful. They wear gloves to avoid prints. But they're not perfect. They make mistakes."

"And you think this mistake is going to lead us to them."

"I think it's a start. The glove has oil stains, grease, particulates. Tommy's running analysis now. If we can identify the source, we can narrow down where the Ghost works."

"Locksmith shops."

"Or repair shops. Anywhere that uses tools and lubricants."

Ortiz leaned back in his chair, arms crossed. "Sienna, I need you to be realistic about this case. We've been chasing the Ghost for weeks. We've got footage, patterns, a geographic profile. But we don't have a name. We don't have a face. And we're running out of time."

"I know."

"Do you? Because from where I'm sitting, it looks like you're getting too invested. This isn't a high-priority case. It's a PR problem that city hall wants resolved. And if we can't resolve it soon, they're going to pull the plug."

Sienna felt her frustration rising. "Captain, with all due respect, this is more than a PR problem. The Ghost has saved twenty-two animals in six months. Twenty-two lives that the system failed to protect. That's not just vigilantism. That's a systemic failure."

"I agree. But that doesn't change the reality. We have limited resources. I can't justify keeping a full task force on this case indefinitely."

"So what are you saying?"

"I'm saying you've got one more week. If you can't ID the Ghost by then, we're scaling back. You and Cole can keep working it on the side, but the task force is done."

Sienna stared at him. One week. Seven days to find someone who'd been operating in the shadows for six months.

"Understood," she said.

Ortiz's expression softened slightly. "For what it's worth, I think you're doing good work. But good work doesn't always lead to results. And results are what city hall cares about."

Sienna stood, picked up the evidence bag. She paused at the door, turned back.

"Captain, can I ask you something?"

"Sure."

"Do you think the Ghost is doing the right thing?"

Ortiz was quiet for a moment. "I think the Ghost is doing what they believe is necessary. But that doesn't make it legal. And it doesn't make it right."

"What if the system is broken? What if the Ghost is the only one filling the gaps?"

"Then we fix the system. Not by breaking the law, but by changing it."

Sienna nodded, but she didn't believe him. Changing the system took years. And in the meantime, animals suffered. And people like the Ghost stepped in to do what the system couldn't.

She left the office, walked back to the war room, and stared at the whiteboard.

One week.

She was going to make it count.

That afternoon, Sienna sat in the coffee shop on Fifth, waiting for Cole. He arrived carrying his laptop, slid into the booth across from her.

"What've you got?" she asked.

Cole turned the laptop toward her. "I've been going through the locksmith businesses in the target zone. There are twelve of them. Most are small operations. But one of them stands out."

He pulled up a business listing. **Brennan's Restoration Shop**. The address was in the heart of the west side, right in the center of the geographic profile.

"Restoration shop," Sienna said. "Not a locksmith."

"But they do lock work. Furniture restoration, antique repair, and lock replacement. I called them, pretended I needed a lock fixed. The guy who answered said they had someone on staff who specialized in locks."

Sienna felt her pulse quicken. "Did you get a name?"

"No. But I got an address. And it's worth checking out."

Sienna stared at the screen. Brennan's Restoration Shop. It was a lead. Maybe the lead.

"Let's go," she said.

Brennan's Restoration Shop was a small storefront wedged between a laundromat and a bodega. The windows were dusty, the sign faded. Sienna and Cole parked across the street, watched the entrance.

"You want to go in?" Cole asked.

"Not yet. Let's see who comes and goes first."

They waited. Ten minutes. Twenty. Then the door opened, and a man stepped out. Mid-twenties, average build, wearing a hoodie and jeans. He had a backpack slung over one shoulder, hands in his pockets, head down.

Sienna's breath caught.

"That could be him," she said.

Cole leaned forward. "Hard to tell from here. But the build matches."

The man walked down the street, turned the corner, and disappeared.

Sienna pulled out her phone, took a photo of the storefront. "We need to come back. Talk to the owner. See if we can get a name."

"And if it's the Ghost?"

Sienna didn't answer. She was staring at the storefront, her mind racing.

One week. She had one week to find the Ghost.

And she was getting closer.

Even if she didn't know what she'd do when she found them.

Chapter 13
Tools of the Trade

Kai stood outside Eli's workshop at 11:47 p.m., staring at the darkened windows. The workshop was in the industrial zone, tucked between a metalworking shop and a warehouse that had been abandoned for years. The sign above the door read **ELI'S LOCKS & KEYS** in faded letters.

Eli Brennan was the closest thing Kai had to a mentor. He'd taught Kai everything he knew about locks—the mechanics, the theory, the art of it. But Eli was also careful. Cautious. The kind of person who didn't ask questions but noticed everything.

And Kai was about to ask him for tools that would raise questions.

He pulled out his phone, sent a text.

You still up?

The reply came thirty seconds later.

Back door. It's open.

The workshop smelled like metal and oil. Eli was at his bench, hunched over a disassembled lock, a jeweler's loupe magnifying his view. He was in his sixties, gray-haired, with hands that moved with the precision of a surgeon. He didn't look up when Kai walked in.

"Late night visit," Eli said, his voice gravelly. "Must be important."

"I need some tools," Kai said.

"You've got tools."

"I need better ones."

Eli set down the lock, removed the loupe, and turned to face Kai. His expression was unreadable. "Better how?"

Kai hesitated. "Specialty picks. Bypass tools. Something that works faster on newer locks."

"You working a job?"

"Something like that."

"Something legal?"

Kai didn't answer.

Eli leaned back against the bench, crossed his arms. "You know, when you first came to me, you were just a kid. Wanted to learn the trade because your father used to do it. I taught you because I saw something in you. Discipline. Respect for the craft. But now..." He trailed off, shook his head. "Now I'm not so sure."

"I'm still the same person," Kai said.

"Are you? Because the person I trained wouldn't be asking for tools like this at midnight." Eli paused. "I've been reading the news, Kai. The Ghost Rescuer. Breaking into cars, freeing animals. It's all over the city."

Kai felt his stomach drop. "I don't know what you're talking about."

"Don't insult me. I know locksmith work when I see it. And I know your work specifically. The precision. The care. The way you leave no damage." Eli's expression softened slightly. "I'm not saying what you're doing is wrong. I'm saying it's dangerous."

Kai met his gaze. "So you're not going to help me."

Eli sighed, stood, and walked to a cabinet in the back of the workshop. He pulled out a small wooden box, set it on the bench, and opened it. Inside were tools Kai had never seen before—picks with unusual angles, tension wrenches with offset handles, bypass tools designed for specific lock types.

"I didn't say that," Eli said quietly.

He picked up one of the picks, held it up to the light. "This one's for wafer locks. This one's for sidebar mechanisms. And this one"—he set it down carefully—"is for when you don't have time to be subtle."

Kai stared at the tools, his pulse quickening. These were exactly what he needed. Faster. More efficient. Better.

"How much?" he asked.

Eli closed the box. "Nothing. But I want to know what you're using them for."

"I can't tell you that."

"Then I can't give them to you."

Kai felt his frustration rising. "Eli—"

"Listen to me, Kai." Eli's voice was firm, but not unkind. "I've been doing this for forty years. I know when someone's working a legitimate job and when they're not. And whatever you're doing, it's not legitimate."

Kai didn't respond.

"You're good. Better than most people I've trained. But good doesn't mean invisible. Locks are clean. You can pick them without leaving a trace. That's the art of it. But cameras? Cameras aren't clean. And if you're doing what I think you're doing, you're leaving a trail."

"I'm careful," Kai said.

"Careful isn't enough. You think you can outsmart surveillance?" Eli shook his head. "I've seen this before. People who think they're smarter than the system. And you know what happens to them? They get caught. Every single time."

"I'm not like them," Kai said.

"No, you're worse. Because you're doing this for the right reasons. And that makes you reckless." Eli picked up one of the tools, turned it over in his hands. "When you believe you're doing the right thing, you take risks you shouldn't. You push harder than you should. You ignore the warning signs. And sooner or later, those risks catch up to you."

"So what am I supposed to do? Just stop? Let the animals suffer?"

"I'm not saying stop. I'm saying be smart. And right now, you're not being smart. You're being idealistic. And idealism gets people arrested."

"Better arrested than complicit," Kai said.

Eli looked at him for a long moment, then sighed. "You sound just like your father."

Kai stared at the box. He knew Eli was right. The alarm at the warehouse. The glove in the stairwell. The footage from the parking garage. Each one a breadcrumb leading back to him.

But the alternative—stopping—felt impossible.

"I need them," Kai said quietly.

Eli studied him, then sighed. "You're not going to listen to me, are you?"

"No."

"Stubborn. Just like your father." Eli picked up the box, held it out to Kai. "Don't let it cost you too."

Kai took the box, felt the weight of it in his hands. "Thank you."

"Don't thank me. Just be smart. And when this catches up to you —and it will—don't say I didn't warn you."

Kai walked back to his apartment, the box tucked under his arm, Eli's words echoing in his head. *Cameras aren't clean. You're leaving a trail.*

By the time he got home, it was past midnight. He dropped the box on the kitchen table, opened it, and spread the tools out. They were beautiful. Precise. Efficient.

With these, he could work faster. Cleaner. Better.

He picked up one of the picks, tested the weight, the balance. It felt right. Like an extension of his hand.

He thought about the parking garage. The forty-seven seconds between freedom and arrest. With these tools, he could cut that time in half. Maybe more.

But Eli's warning lingered. *You think you can outsmart surveillance?*

Kai set the pick down, pulled out his notebook, and started writing.

New Tools:

- Wafer lock pick: faster entry on commercial vehicles

- Sidebar bypass: works on newer car models

- Tension wrench (offset): better leverage on tight mechanisms

Advantages:

- Speed: cuts lock time by 30-50%

- Precision: less chance of scratching or damaging locks

Risks:

- Custom tools = identifiable if recovered

- Faster doesn't mean invisible

- Cameras still a problem

He stared at the list, jaw tight. The tools would help. But they wouldn't solve the fundamental problem: he was being hunted.

He closed the notebook, stood, and walked to the window. The city stretched out below him, a grid of lights and shadows. Somewhere out there, animals were suffering. Trapped. Forgotten.

And Kai could hear them. He always could.

He pulled out his phone, opened the notes app, and scrolled through the list of targets he'd been tracking. Three locations. Three opportunities.

He could stop. Walk away.

Or he could keep going. Smarter. Faster. Better.

He thought about Eli's warning. *When this catches up to you— and it will—don't say I didn't warn you.*

Kai grabbed his jacket and headed for the door.

He wasn't going to stop.

The first target was a house on the edge of the industrial zone. Kai had been watching it for three days. A dog chained in the backyard, no shelter, no water. The owner left for work at 7 a.m., came home at 6 p.m. Eleven hours a day alone, exposed to the elements, the chain barely long enough to reach the shade.

The signal had been constant for days—a low, persistent ache that never quite faded. Thirst. Hunger. Loneliness.

Kai arrived at 8 p.m., parked two blocks away, and walked the rest of the distance. The house was dark. The street was quiet. The backyard was accessible through a side gate, padlocked but simple.

He pulled out the new tools, selected the wafer lock pick, and went to work. The lock opened in under ten seconds—smooth, clean, no resistance. Eli's tools were as good as promised.

Kai slipped into the backyard, moving quickly. The dog was there, chained to a post, lying in the dirt. It looked up when Kai approached, ears flat, tail tucked. Scared but not aggressive. Just tired.

Kai crouched, held out his hand. The dog sniffed, hesitated, then licked his fingers. Its tongue was dry, rough.

"I know," Kai said quietly. "I'm here to help."

He examined the chain. It was padlocked to the dog's collar, heavy-duty lock, weatherproof casing. The kind that said *I don't care if this animal suffers.*

Kai pulled out the sidebar bypass, worked the lock, and felt it give way with a satisfying click. The chain fell to the ground with a dull thud.

The dog stood, shook itself, and looked at Kai with wide eyes. For a moment, it didn't move, as if it couldn't believe it was free.

"Go," Kai said, pointing toward the gate. "You're free."

The dog hesitated, then bolted. It ran through the gate, down the street, disappearing into the night. Kai watched it go, felt the signal fade, replaced by something lighter. Relief. Freedom.

He stood, pocketed the tools, and left the same way he'd come. No note this time. No water. Just the chain, lying in the dirt, and the empty space where the dog had been.

Ten seconds on the gate. Fifteen on the chain. Twenty-five seconds total.

But Eli's words still echoed in his head. *You're leaving a trail.*

Kai pulled his hood tighter and kept walking.

The second target was a storage facility. Kai had seen the reports on social media—cats trapped inside a locked unit, crying for days. The facility had security cameras, but they were old, poorly maintained. Kai had scouted the location twice, mapped the blind spots, and timed the security guard's rounds.

He arrived at 10 p.m., hood up, hands in pockets. The facility was quiet, the parking lot mostly empty. Kai moved through the blind spots and reached the unit.

The lock was a standard pin tumbler, easy to pick. But the unit was alarmed. Kai could see the sensor on the door frame.

He pulled out the offset tension wrench, worked the lock, and felt it turn. Then he reached up, carefully peeled back the sensor, and opened the door just enough to slip inside.

The smell hit him immediately—ammonia, feces, decay. The unit was dark, cluttered with boxes and furniture. And in the corner, huddled together, were three cats.

Kai crouched, pulled out his penlight, and approached slowly. The cats hissed, backed away, but didn't run. They were too weak, too scared.

He pulled out the collapsible water bottle, poured water into the cap, and set it on the ground. The cats approached cautiously, sniffed, then drank.

Kai stood, walked back to the door, and propped it open. Then he stepped outside, closed the unit behind him, and walked away.

The cats would find their way out. And someone would notice the open door.

He was getting better at this. Faster. More precise.

But the cameras had seen him. He knew that. Even in the blind spots, there were angles. Reflections. Shadows.

Eli was right. He was leaving a trail.

By the time Kai got home, it was past midnight. He dropped onto the futon, exhausted, wired, caught between the thrill of success and the fear of consequences.

He pulled out his notebook, added two more entries to the list. Twenty-four rescues now.

The net was tightening. He could feel it.

He thought about Eli's warning. *When this catches up to you—and it will—don't say I didn't warn you.*

Kai closed the notebook.

He knew he was running out of time. He knew the police were getting closer. He knew that every rescue brought him one step closer to arrest.

But he couldn't stop.

Because the signals wouldn't stop. And neither would the suffering.

And as long as there were animals out there, trapped in the gaps the system left behind, Kai DuMoire would keep going.

Even if it meant getting caught.

Even if it meant losing everything.

Because some things were worth the risk.

And this was one of them.

Chapter 14
Pressure from Above

Sienna arrived at the precinct at 7:30 a.m., coffee in hand, ready to dive into the forensics reports Tommy had promised. But before she could reach her desk, Cole intercepted her in the hallway.

"Ortiz wants to see you," he said. "Now."

Sienna felt her stomach tighten. "What's this about?"

"City Hall. The Ghost. The usual." Cole's expression was grim. "Good luck."

* * *

Captain Ortiz's office was on the third floor, overlooking the parking lot. It was a small space, cluttered with files and commendations. Ortiz was behind his desk, reading something on his computer, his jaw tight. ADA Lee was sitting across from him, arms crossed.

"Close the door," Ortiz said without looking up.

Sienna closed the door, took the empty chair beside Lee. "What's going on?"

Ortiz turned the monitor toward her. On the screen was an

article from *The Signal Line*, published that morning. The headline read: **"Ghost Rescuer Strikes Again: Police Still Searching."**

Sienna scanned the article. Written by Mina Torres. Two new rescues—a dog freed from a chain, three cats released from a storage unit. Both within the past twenty-four hours. Both with the Ghost's signature: no damage, no confrontation, clean extraction.

But what caught Sienna's attention was the tone. Mina wasn't just reporting facts—she was framing them. The article painted the Ghost as a necessary response to systemic failure, asking pointed questions about why the police hadn't prevented the suffering in the first place.

"Twenty-four rescues now," Ortiz said. "And we're no closer to catching them than we were a month ago."

"That's not true," Sienna said. "We've got forensic evidence. We've got a geographic profile. We've narrowed the search to a two-square-mile zone. We've identified the tools, the lubricant on their gloves, and we've got a lead on a restoration shop—"

"It's not enough," Lee interrupted. "City Hall is getting hammered from both sides. Activists are holding the Ghost up as a hero. Liability lawyers are warning about copycats. And the mayor's office is demanding results."

"We're working on it."

"Not fast enough." Lee pulled out his phone, scrolled, then turned the screen toward Sienna. "Do you know how many calls we've gotten in the past week? Fifty-three. People reporting animals in distress, demanding to know why the police aren't responding as fast as the Ghost. Social media is exploding. There are hashtags. Fundraisers. People are calling the Ghost a folk hero."

"Maybe they're right," Sienna said quietly.

Lee's expression hardened. "Excuse me?"

"Maybe the Ghost is filling a gap the system can't. Maybe people are responding because they see someone actually doing something."

Lee leaned forward. "Detective Halbrook, I don't care what the public thinks. I care about liability. Do you know what happens if someone gets hurt trying to imitate the Ghost? If a copycat breaks into the wrong car and gets shot? The city is liable. And the Ghost is the catalyst."

"The Ghost isn't the problem. The system is."

"That's not the point. The point is that vigilantism, regardless of intent, creates legal and public safety risks. And it's our job to stop it."

Sienna felt her frustration rising. "So what do you want me to do? Arrest someone for saving lives?"

"I want you to do your job. Which is to enforce the law."

Ortiz held up a hand. "Enough. Both of you." He turned to Sienna. "Lee's right. The pressure is coming from above. But he's also right that we need to be smart about this. If we catch the Ghost, we need to do it cleanly. No mistakes. No media circus."

"And if we don't catch them?"

"Then we scale back and move on. But that's not the outcome anyone wants."

Sienna stared at him. "You're giving up."

"I'm being realistic. We've got limited resources and unlimited problems. I can't justify keeping a full task force on this indefinitely."

"So what are you saying?"

"I'm saying you've got one more week. If you can't ID the Ghost by then, we're pulling the plug. You and Cole can keep working it on the side, but the task force is done."

Sienna felt her jaw tighten. One week. Again.

"What about resources? Can I get more surveillance? More forensics support?"

Ortiz glanced at Lee, who shook his head.

"We're stretched thin as it is. You've got what you've got."

Sienna stood. "Is that all?"

"One more thing," Ortiz said. "The mayor's office wants a press conference. They want to reassure the public that we're taking this seriously. I need you to be there."

"When?"

"Tomorrow. Noon."

Sienna nodded and walked out.

By the time Sienna got back to the war room, she was seething. She dropped into her chair, stared at the whiteboard.

Cole walked in, carrying two cups of coffee. He set one on her desk. "How'd it go?"

"About as well as you'd expect."

"Ortiz pull the plug?"

"Not yet. But he's close. We've got one more week. After that, we're on our own."

"We're already on our own. Ortiz has been phoning it in since day one. Lee cares more about liability than justice. And City Hall just wants the problem to go away."

"So what do we do?"

Cole leaned against the desk, arms crossed. "We follow the evidence. We build the case. And we catch the Ghost."

Sienna stared at the whiteboard. The map. The red dots. The timeline. Everything pointed to a single operator with specialized skills and a clear moral framework. Someone who cared enough to risk everything.

Someone she was starting to admire, even as she hunted them.

"I need to talk to Tommy. See if he's got anything on the glove."

"Already checked. He's in the lab."

Tommy was at his workstation, surrounded by monitors and evidence bags. He looked up when Sienna walked in.

"Got something for you," he said, pulling up a file. "The glove. DNA came back negative—no match in the system. But the particulates are interesting."

"How interesting?"

"Very. The oil on the glove is a specific blend—locksmith lubricant, used for pin tumbler mechanisms. It's specialty stuff, the kind locksmiths order in bulk."

Sienna felt her pulse quicken. "Can you trace it?"

"Already did. Three suppliers in the region. I cross-referenced them with the geographic profile, and one stands out." Tommy pulled up a map, highlighted a location. "Brennan's Restoration Shop. They order locksmith supplies regularly. And they're right in the center of your target zone."

Sienna stared at the screen. Brennan's. The same shop she and Cole had staked out two days ago.

"We need to go back."

"Already ahead of you. I pulled the business records. The shop is owned by Eli Brennan, sixty-three, been in business for forty years. But he's got an employee—part-time, off the books. Neighbors say there's a younger guy who works there sometimes. Mid-twenties, quiet, keeps to himself."

"That's our Ghost."

"Maybe. But you're going to need more than 'maybe' to get a warrant."

Sienna thought for a moment. "What if we go in as customers? Ask about lock services, see who's working there?"

"That could work. But if the Ghost is there, they might recognize you. You've been all over the news."

"Then I'll send Cole."

Tommy nodded. "Smart. But be careful."

That afternoon, Sienna sat in the war room, staring at the map. Brennan's Restoration Shop. Locksmith lubricant. A part-time employee who matched the Ghost's description.

It was all circumstantial. But it was the closest they'd gotten.

Her phone buzzed. A text from Cole.

At Brennan's. Shop's open. Eli Brennan is here. No sign of the younger guy.

Sienna typed a reply.

Ask about lock services. See if he mentions anyone else.

She waited. Five minutes. Ten.

Another text.

Eli says he's got someone who does lock work. Didn't give a name. Said he's not in today. Offered to call him if I need something urgent.

Sienna felt her heart race.

Get the number.

Another pause.

He won't give it. Says the guy values his privacy. But he did say he'll be in tomorrow morning.

Sienna set the phone down. Tomorrow morning. Less than twenty-four hours.

That evening, Sienna sat in her apartment, the case files spread across her kitchen table. Photos of the Ghost's interventions. Forensic reports. Timelines. Maps. Twenty-four rescues. Twenty-four animals that would have died without intervention.

She thought about what Lee had said. *It's our job to enforce the law.*

But what if the law was failing? What if the system was broken, and the Ghost was the only one filling the gaps?

Sienna had joined the force because she believed in justice. She believed that the system, for all its flaws, was better than chaos.

But the Ghost wasn't chaos. The Ghost wasn't hurting anyone. They were saving lives. Quietly. Efficiently. Without recognition or reward.

And the system—the system Sienna had sworn to uphold—was failing to do the same.

She picked up one of the photos. The golden retriever from the parking garage. The water bottle left on the seat. The precision. The care.

The Ghost wasn't a criminal. Not really. They were someone

who saw suffering and couldn't look away. Someone who had the skills to act and the courage to use them.

Someone Sienna was starting to understand, even as she hunted them.

And that scared her.

She closed the case file and walked to the window. The city stretched out below her, a grid of lights and shadows. Somewhere out there, the Ghost was planning their next move. And Sienna was planning hers.

But for the first time since this case began, she wasn't sure she wanted to catch them.

Tomorrow, they would meet. Not face-to-face. But close enough.

And when they did, Sienna would have to decide: was she going to arrest the Ghost, or let them go?

She didn't know the answer.

The next morning, Sienna and Cole sat in an unmarked car across the street from Brennan's Restoration Shop. It was 8:45 a.m., fifteen minutes before the shop opened. The street was quiet.

"You think he'll show?" Cole asked.

"He'll show. He has to."

They waited. 8:50. 9:00. The shop lights turned on. Eli Brennan appeared in the window, unlocking the door.

9:15. A figure appeared at the end of the block, walking toward the shop. Mid-twenties, average build, wearing a hoodie and jeans. He had a backpack slung over one shoulder, hands in his pockets, head down.

Sienna's breath caught.

"That's him," she said.

Cole leaned forward. "You sure?"

"Look at the way he moves. The posture. The gait. It matches the footage."

The figure reached the shop, paused at the door, then stepped inside.

Sienna pulled out her phone, took a photo. Then she opened the DMV database, started cross-referencing.

"Got him," she said. "Kai DuMoire. Twenty-six. Lives on the west side. No priors. Works part-time at Brennan's."

Cole stared at the shop. "That's the Ghost."

"Yeah," Sienna said. "That's the Ghost."

She sat back, stared at the photo on her phone. Kai DuMoire. The Ghost Rescuer. The person she'd been hunting for weeks.

And now she had a name.

Now she had to decide what to do with it.

Chapter 15
The Copycat

Mina's phone rang at 6:47 a.m., jolting her awake. She fumbled for it, squinting at the screen. Her editor, Raj.

"Please tell me you're awake," Raj said without preamble.

"I am now."

"Good. We've got a situation. Kid tried to break into a car last night, said he was 'doing what the Ghost does.' Broke a window, triggered an alarm, got arrested. It's all over the police scanner."

Mina sat up, suddenly alert. "A copycat?"

"Looks like it. And ADA Lee is already calling for a press conference. This is big, Mina. I need you on it."

"Where's the kid now?"

"Juvenile detention. But his mother's willing to talk. I'll text you the address."

Mina was out of bed before the call ended.

The house was in a quiet neighborhood on the south side, a modest single-story with a chain-link fence. Mina knocked on the door, notebook in hand.

The woman who answered was in her forties, tired-looking, with red-rimmed eyes. "You're the reporter?"

"Mina Torres. Thank you for agreeing to talk."

The woman nodded, stepped aside. "Come in."

The living room was small, cluttered with family photos. Mina sat on the couch, pulled out her recorder. "Can I get your name?"

"Angela Martinez. My son is Marcus. He's sixteen."

"Can you tell me what happened?"

Angela sat down across from her, hands clasped tightly. "Marcus has always been a good kid. He volunteers at the animal shelter on weekends. Last night, he saw a dog locked in a car outside a grocery store. The windows were cracked, but it was hot, and the dog was panting. Marcus waited for the owner, but they didn't come. So he..." She trailed off, shook her head. "He tried to break the window. To save the dog."

"And he got arrested," Mina said gently.

"The alarm went off. The owner came running out, called the police. Marcus tried to explain, but they didn't care. They arrested him for vandalism and attempted theft." Angela's voice cracked. "He was just trying to help. He thought he was doing the right thing."

"Did he mention the Ghost?"

Angela nodded. "He's been following the story. Reading your articles. He said if the Ghost could do it, so could he. He thought he was being a hero."

Mina felt her stomach tighten. "I'm sorry."

"It's not your fault," Angela said, but her tone suggested otherwise. "But people are listening to what you write. And kids like Marcus—they don't understand the difference between someone who knows what they're doing and someone who doesn't."

Mina thanked Angela, left the house, and sat in her car, staring at her notes.

Marcus Martinez. Sixteen. Arrested for trying to be a hero.

And Mina had helped create the myth that inspired him.

By the time Mina got to the newsroom, the story was already exploding. ADA Lee had called a press conference. Mina pulled up the stream on her laptop, watched as Lee stood at a podium, flanked by Captain Ortiz and the mayor.

"Last night, a sixteen-year-old boy was arrested for attempting to break into a vehicle," Lee said. "He told police he was inspired by the so-called Ghost Rescuer. This is exactly the kind of dangerous behavior we've been warning about. Vigilantism, regardless of intent, creates public safety risks. It inspires copycats."

The camera cut to a reporter. "Do you hold the Ghost responsible for this incident?"

"Absolutely. The Ghost has created a narrative that breaking the law is acceptable if you believe you're doing the right thing. That narrative is dangerous. And it's our responsibility to stop it before someone gets seriously hurt."

Mina closed the laptop, leaned back. Lee was right. The Ghost had created a narrative. But Mina had amplified it. She'd turned the Ghost into a folk hero. And now a kid was paying the price.

Raj walked over, set a cup of coffee on her desk. "You okay?"

"No."

"Yeah, I figured." He pulled up a chair. "Look, I know this is hard. But you didn't make that kid break a window. He made that choice."

"I made him think it was the right choice," Mina said.

"Maybe. Or maybe the system made him think it was the right choice. You're not responsible for every person who reads your work and decides to act on it."

"Aren't I? I framed the Ghost as a hero. I asked why the police weren't doing more. I made it sound like the Ghost was the only one who cared. And now a sixteen-year-old kid has a criminal record because he believed me."

Raj was quiet. "So what are you going to do?"

"I don't know."

"Well, you need to figure it out. Because Lee just made this story even bigger. And people are going to want your take on it."

Mina spent the morning interviewing sources. Activists who defended Marcus. Lawyers who argued he should be charged. Shelter workers who understood his intent but questioned his methods. By noon, she had enough material for an article. But she didn't know how to write it.

She opened a blank document, stared at the cursor.

When Heroes Inspire Trouble

Deleted.

The Cost of Inspiration

Deleted again.

What Happens When Myths Become Reality

She stared at the screen. The Ghost had started as a story about systemic failure. But now it was something else. A symbol. A call to action that had inspired a sixteen-year-old to get arrested.

She thought about Angela Martinez, voice breaking. *He thought he was being a hero.*

She thought about the Ghost, somewhere out there, realizing their myth had escaped control.

She thought about her own role. The articles she'd written. The narrative she'd built.

And she started typing.

When Heroes Inspire Trouble

By Mina Torres

Last night, a sixteen-year-old boy named Marcus Martinez was arrested for attempting to break into a vehicle. He told police he was trying to save a dog locked inside. He also said he was inspired by the Ghost Rescuer—the vigilante who has become a folk hero in this city over the past six months.

Marcus broke a window. He triggered an alarm. He was arrested, charged with vandalism and attempted theft. And now he has a criminal record.

This is the cost of inspiration.

The Ghost Rescuer has saved twenty-four animals in six months. Each rescue has been clean, efficient, and effective. But Marcus Martinez is not the Ghost. He's a sixteen-year-old kid who saw suffering and wanted to help. And he didn't have the skills or the knowledge to do it safely.

ADA Lee is right: the Ghost has created a narrative that breaking the law is acceptable if you believe you're doing the right thing. And that narrative is dangerous.

But here's the uncomfortable truth: the Ghost wouldn't exist if the system was working. Marcus Martinez wouldn't have felt compelled to act if he believed the authorities would respond. And this city wouldn't be divided over a vigilante if we weren't all grappling with the same question: what do we do when the system fails?

The Ghost is not a hero. The Ghost is a symptom. A symptom of a system that is stretched too thin, underfunded, and overwhelmed. A system that leaves animals suffering in locked cars while emergency services are tied up with higher-priority calls.

Marcus Martinez made a choice. It was the wrong choice, executed poorly, with consequences he didn't anticipate. But it was a choice born from the same frustration that created the Ghost in the first place.

So yes, the Ghost is responsible. But so are we. All of us. For allowing a system to fail so completely that a vigilante becomes necessary. For celebrating that vigilante without acknowledging the risks. For building a myth without considering the cost.

The Ghost has inspired people. But inspiration without guidance is dangerous. And until we fix the system that made the Ghost necessary, we're going to keep seeing stories like Marcus Martinez.

The question is: are we willing to do the work?

Mina stopped typing, read through the article twice, then hit send.

The article went live at 3 p.m. By 5 p.m., it had been shared over two thousand times. The comments were split. Some agreed with her. Others accused her of blaming the Ghost for systemic failure. A few called her a hypocrite for building the myth and then criticizing it.

They weren't wrong.

Mina sat at her desk, scrolling through responses, feeling the weight of every word she'd written. She'd started this story because she believed it mattered. Because she thought the Ghost was exposing something important.

But now she wasn't sure.

Her phone buzzed. A text from an unknown number.

You're right. The Ghost is a symptom. But symptoms don't fix themselves. Someone has to act. Even when it's dangerous. Even when it's illegal. Because the alternative is doing nothing. And doing nothing is worse.

Mina stared at the message. It wasn't signed. But she knew who it was from.

The Ghost.

She set the phone down, leaned back.

The Ghost was right. Someone had to act. But acting had consequences. And Mina was starting to realize that she was part of those consequences.

She'd built the myth. And now she had to live with what it had become.

. . .

Across the city, Kai sat on his futon, staring at Mina's article on his phone. He'd read it three times, each word hitting harder than the last.

Marcus Martinez. Sixteen. Arrested.

Kai felt sick.

He'd known this was a risk. Eli had warned him. Sienna's task force had warned the public. But knowing and seeing were two different things.

A kid had tried to be the Ghost. And now he had a criminal record.

Because of Kai.

He set the phone down, closed his eyes.

The signals were still there, constant and insistent. Animals suffering. Trapped. Forgotten.

But now, every time Kai acted, he wasn't just risking himself. He was inspiring others. And those others didn't have the skills, the caution, the understanding.

He thought about Marcus Martinez, breaking a window, thinking he was doing the right thing.

He thought about Angela Martinez, trying to explain why her son was in detention.

He thought about Mina Torres, writing articles that framed him as a hero, even as she questioned what that heroism cost.

And he thought about himself. Kai DuMoire. Locksmith. Nobody. The person who'd started all of this because he couldn't ignore the signals.

The Ghost wasn't just him anymore. It was a movement. A symbol. A myth that had taken on a life of its own.

And Kai didn't know how to stop it.

Or if he even should.

Because the signals were still there. And the animals were still suffering.

And someone had to act.

Even if it meant more Marcus Martinezes. Even if it meant more consequences.

Because the alternative was doing nothing.

And doing nothing was worse.

Kai stood, grabbed his jacket, and headed for the door.

The Ghost had work to do.

Chapter 16
The Lead

Sienna was staring at the whiteboard when Tommy walked into the war room, laptop under his arm, expression grim.

"Got something," he said. "You're going to want to see this."

Sienna turned. "What is it?"

Tommy set his laptop on the table, pulled up a file. "Remember those animal control complaints I was cross-referencing? The ones that never got resolved?"

"Yeah."

"I found a pattern. Seventeen complaints over the past two years, all pointing to the same location. A property on the outskirts of the city, near the industrial zone. But here's the thing—the complaints were filed, logged, and then... nothing. No follow-up. No inspections. No enforcement."

Sienna leaned in. "Why not?"

"Because the property is owned through a shell company. And that shell company is registered to Leonard Grayson."

Sienna felt her pulse quicken. "The Leonard Grayson? City council?"

"The same. Real estate developer, political donor, sits on half a dozen boards. And according to these complaints, he's running an illegal kennel operation on that property."

Sienna pulled up a chair. "What kind of operation?"

"Puppy mill, most likely. The complaints mention overcrowding, unsanitary conditions, animals in distress. But every time animal control tries to follow up, they get stonewalled. Grayson's lawyers threaten lawsuits. The city backs off."

"And the animals?"

"Still there. As far as I can tell, nothing's changed."

Sienna stared at the screen. Seventeen complaints. Two years. And nothing done.

"Do we have an address?"

Tommy pulled up a map, highlighted a location. "Here. About twenty miles outside the city. Remote. Fenced. No neighbors within a mile."

"Perfect place to hide something."

Sienna stood, walked to the whiteboard, and added a new pin to the map. Leonard Grayson's property. The biggest lead they'd had in weeks.

"We need to get eyes on this," she said.

"Agreed. But you're going to need a warrant. And getting a warrant on Leonard Grayson is going to be... complicated."

"I know."

An hour later, Sienna sat in Captain Ortiz's office, the case file spread out on his desk. Ortiz was reading through the complaints, his expression darkening with each page.

"Seventeen complaints," he said finally. "And no one followed up?"

"Grayson's lawyers shut it down every time. Threatened lawsuits, claimed the complaints were harassment. Animal control backed off."

"And you think this is connected to the Ghost?"

"I think this is exactly the kind of case the Ghost would target. Remote location. Systemic failure. Animals suffering with no one willing to act."

Ortiz leaned back in his chair, arms crossed. "You want a warrant."

"I want surveillance first. Get eyes on the property, confirm the complaints. Then we go for a warrant."

"And if Grayson finds out we're watching him?"

"Then we deal with it. But we can't ignore this, Captain. If the complaints are accurate, there are animals suffering out there right now. And if we don't act, the Ghost will."

Ortiz was quiet. "Grayson has friends in City Hall. If this goes sideways, it's not just your badge on the line. It's mine too."

"I know."

"And you still want to do this."

"I have to."

Ortiz sighed. "All right. But you do this quietly. Skeleton crew. No media. And if Grayson's lawyers get wind of it, you shut it down immediately. Understood?"

"Understood."

That afternoon, Sienna sat in the war room with Cole and Tommy, planning the surveillance operation. They'd pulled up satellite images of Grayson's property—a large compound with multiple buildings, fenced perimeter, and a gated entrance.

"We'll need at least two vantage points," Cole said, pointing to the map. "One here, on the access road. One here, on the ridge overlooking the property."

"What about cameras?" Sienna asked.

"I can set up remote feeds," Tommy said. "Motion-activated, night vision. If anything moves, we'll see it."

"How long will it take to set up?"

"A few hours. But we'll need to do it at night."

Sienna nodded. "We go tonight. Cole, you're with me. Tommy, you coordinate from here. If we see anything that confirms the complaints, we move for a warrant."

That evening, Sienna sat in her apartment, staring at the case file. Seventeen complaints. Two years. Animals suffering with no one willing to act.

She thought about the Ghost. About Kai DuMoire, working alone, filling the gaps the system left behind. She'd spent weeks hunting him, building a case. But now, staring at Leonard Grayson's file, she understood why he did it.

Because the system was failing. And someone had to act.

Her phone buzzed. A text from Cole.

Ready when you are.

Sienna grabbed her jacket and headed for the door.

The drive to Grayson's property took forty minutes. By the time they arrived, it was past midnight. The access road was dark, unpaved, winding through dense trees. Sienna parked the unmarked car a quarter mile from the property, killed the lights, and stepped out.

The air was cool, thick with the smell of pine and damp earth. They moved quietly, staying off the road, using the tree line for cover.

Ten minutes later, they reached the ridge overlooking the property. Sienna pulled out her binoculars, scanned the compound.

The main building was large, industrial-looking, with corrugated metal siding. Behind it were two smaller structures. The entire property was surrounded by a chain-link fence topped with barbed wire.

"Looks more like a prison than a kennel," Cole said quietly.

Sienna focused on the main building. She could hear something —faint, distant, but unmistakable.

Barking.

Lots of it.

"You hear that?" she asked.

Cole nodded. "Yeah. There are dogs in there. A lot of them."

Sienna lowered the binoculars, pulled out her phone, and took a photo. Then she turned to Cole. "Set up the cameras. I want full coverage."

Cole nodded, opened the duffel bag, and started assembling the equipment. Sienna watched the compound, listening to the barking, feeling the weight of what they were about to uncover.

By 2 a.m., the cameras were in place. Sienna and Cole returned to the car, set up the remote feeds on Tommy's laptop, and started monitoring.

At 2:17 a.m., a truck pulled up to the gate. The driver got out, unlocked it, and drove through. The truck parked near the main building, and two men stepped out. They opened the back, pulled out several crates, and carried them inside.

Sienna leaned forward. "What's in those crates?"

"Can't tell from here," Cole said. "But if I had to guess? More dogs."

Sienna felt her jaw tighten. "We need to get closer."

"Sienna—"

"I know. Surveillance only. But we're not going to see anything from up here. I need to know what's inside that building."

Cole was quiet. "If we get caught, Ortiz is going to kill us."

"Then we don't get caught."

They approached the compound on foot, moving slowly, staying low. The fence was too high to climb, but there was a section near the back where the barbed wire had been cut. Sienna slipped through, Cole following close behind.

The barking was louder now, echoing off the metal walls. Sienna moved toward it, staying in the shadows. She reached the side of the building, found a window, and peered inside.

What she saw made her stomach turn.

The building was filled with cages. Dozens of them, stacked floor to ceiling, each one holding a dog. The conditions were horrific—overcrowded, filthy, no ventilation. Some of the dogs were barking, others were silent, lying in their own waste. The smell, even from outside, was overwhelming.

Sienna pulled out her phone, took photos. Then she turned to Cole, her voice tight. "We've got enough. Let's go."

They slipped back through the fence, returned to the car, and drove away in silence.

By the time they got back to the precinct, it was almost 4 a.m. Tommy was waiting for them in the war room.

"How'd it go?" he asked.

Sienna set her phone on the table, pulled up the photos. "It's worse than we thought. Dozens of dogs. Overcrowded. Filthy. No food, no water. It's a puppy mill. And Grayson's running it."

Tommy stared at the photos. "Jesus."

"We need a warrant," Sienna said. "Now."

"You're going to need more than photos. You're going to need probable cause. And with Grayson's connections, that's going to be hard to get."

"Then we make it easy. We go to ADA Lee. Show her the evidence. Make the case."

The next morning, Sienna sat in ADA Lee's office, the case file spread out on the desk between them. Lee was reading through the complaints, studying the photos, his expression unreadable.

"This is Leonard Grayson," Lee said finally. "City council. Political donor. One of the most connected people in this city."

"I know."

"And you want a warrant to raid his property."

"I want a warrant to investigate credible complaints of animal cruelty. The fact that it's Grayson's property is irrelevant."

Lee set down the file, leaned back. "It's not irrelevant. Grayson has lawyers. Good ones. If we move on this and it falls apart, the city is going to get sued. And you're going to lose your badge."

"And if we don't move, those animals are going to keep suffering."

"That's not my problem."

Sienna felt her frustration rising. "It should be."

Lee's expression hardened. "Detective Halbrook, I understand your passion. But passion doesn't win cases. Evidence does. And right now, all you have are photos taken during an unauthorized surveillance operation. That's not enough for a warrant. And it's definitely not enough to go after someone like Grayson."

"So what do you want me to do? Just walk away?"

"I want you to build a case. Get more evidence. Get witnesses. Get something that will hold up in court. And then we'll talk about a warrant."

Sienna stood. "How long is that going to take?"

"As long as it takes."

"And in the meantime, those animals suffer."

"That's the reality of the system, Detective. I'm sorry."

Sienna walked out, her jaw tight, her hands shaking. She'd done everything right. Followed procedure. Built a case. And it still wasn't enough.

Because Leonard Grayson had money. And connections. And lawyers.

And the system protected people like him.

· · ·

That afternoon, Sienna sat in the war room, staring at the photos on her laptop. The dogs in the cages. The filth. The suffering.

Cole walked in, set a cup of coffee on her desk. "Lee said no?"

"Lee said not yet. He wants more evidence."

"How much more?"

"Enough to guarantee a conviction. Which means weeks, maybe months."

Cole sat down across from her. "So what are you going to do?"

Sienna didn't answer. She was staring at the photos, thinking about the Ghost. About Kai DuMoire, operating outside the system because the system was failing.

She'd spent weeks hunting him. Judging him. Trying to bring him to justice.

But now she understood.

"I'm going to act," she said quietly.

"What does that mean?"

"It means I'm done waiting for the system to catch up. If Lee won't give me a warrant, I'll find another way."

Cole leaned forward. "Sienna, if you go after Grayson without authorization, you're risking everything. Your badge. Your career. Maybe even criminal charges."

"I know."

"And you're still going to do it."

"I have to."

Cole was quiet. Then he nodded. "All right. Then I'm with you."

Sienna looked at him. "You don't have to—"

"I know. But I'm with you anyway."

Sienna felt something shift inside her. For weeks, she'd been operating within the system, following the rules, trusting that justice would prevail. But the system was broken. And if she wanted to save those animals, she was going to have to break the rules.

Just like the Ghost.

She pulled out her phone, sent a text to Tommy.

DuMoire

*I need everything you have on Grayson's property. Security.
Access points. Schedules. Everything.*

The reply came thirty seconds later.

On it.

Sienna set the phone down, stared at the photos one more time.

She was done hunting the Ghost.

Now she was going to become one.

Chapter 17
The Surveillance
Sienna

Sienna Halbrook sat in her unmarked car, half a block from the warehouse on 38th and Lincoln, watching the entrance through a pair of field binoculars. The building didn't look like much—concrete walls, barred windows, a roll-up door scarred with old graffiti. But it was active. Too active. Lights stayed on past midnight. Deliveries came and went without ever being logged. And she knew the smell by now—urine, bleach, and fear.

She'd been staking out the place for days. Not under official orders. This wasn't an assigned case. This was what she did on suspension. While IA decided her fate.

She was breaking rules again. But this time, she was doing it alone.

A flicker of movement near the side entrance caught her eye. A man with a clipboard opened the door and gestured someone inside. The door shut fast behind them. No cameras visible. No official signage. Just the quiet hum of something terrible continuing out of sight.

She picked up her phone and typed a quick text.

Warehouse. 38th and Lincoln. Definitely active.

She didn't send it. Not yet.

Not to Kai.

She hadn't spoken to him in a week. Not since the last raid. Not since she told him they needed space. That he needed to lie low.

She deleted the text.

Sienna sat back, eyes on the warehouse. She wasn't going to tip him off.

This time, she was going to get the evidence herself.

Kai

Kai crouched on the roof of the old bakery across the street, watching the same warehouse through a cracked skylight. He didn't need binoculars.

He could feel the animals.

Six of them, maybe more. Trapped. Sick. Afraid.

The building reeked of stress. The emotional signature was thick —like walking through fog made of static. And at the center of it: fear. Compacted. Suffocating.

He saw the clipboard man disappear into a side door. Then nothing.

He reached into his jacket, pulled out the hand-sketched map he'd drawn of the interior layout based on thermal scans and prior break-ins. No blueprints available. No records on file.

That's how these places worked. Off-grid. Unlicensed. Disposable.

He could wait for the perfect moment. Or he could act now.

He checked the time. 12:04 AM.

No patrols.

He pulled on gloves, slung his small satchel over his shoulder, and moved toward the alley.

He didn't know that Sienna was watching from the car two buildings down.

He didn't know she'd seen him cross the street.

Chapter 18
Fractures
Sienna

Sienna cursed under her breath as she spotted the dark figure dropping down from the rooftop across the street.

Kai.

Of course it was him.

She reached for the door handle, hesitated. Her instinct screamed to stop him—to pull him out before he got himself arrested. Or worse.

But she didn't move.

She watched instead as he skirted the pool of light cast by the warehouse floodlamp, his steps precise, fluid. Like he'd done this a dozen times.

He had.

Sienna leaned back in her seat and shut her eyes. There was no stopping him. There never had been.

All she could do now was hope he got out clean.

Kai

The lock on the side door was cheap, low-grade steel with a lazy cylinder. It gave in less than ten seconds.

Inside, the warehouse was colder than he expected. Not just in temperature—but in atmosphere. Clinical. Empty. Echoing.

He stepped carefully, hugging the shadowed walls as he moved between tall stacks of unmarked crates. He passed old equipment—unused kennels, stacked pallets, rusting chain.

Then the signal hit him harder.

He paused. Breathed.

The animals were close.

He turned a corner and found the row of holding cages. Six total. Three dogs. Two cats. One ferret. All in varying states of neglect. One of the dogs whimpered as he approached.

Kai knelt, held out a gloved hand. The dog—an old black Lab—wagged her tail weakly, eyes cloudy.

"You're okay," Kai whispered. "I'm getting you out."

He scanned the cages for built-in locks—two were zip-tied, four had padlocks. He reached into his satchel for cutters.

But then: voices. Near the front entrance.

Kai moved fast. Quiet. He ducked behind a stack of pallets, heart pounding in rhythm with the electric buzz of tension rising in the room.

Two men entered, laughing about something—drunk, maybe. One carried a flashlight, the beam slicing through the dark like a blade. The other jiggled keys.

"Shipment leaves tomorrow," one of them muttered. "Boss says we clear out the weak ones tonight. Doesn't want anything dying in transit."

Kai felt nausea twist in his gut.

Clear out.

He couldn't wait.

Sienna

She saw the warehouse door open again—this time from the inside.

Two men stepped out, laughing. No sign of Kai.

Sienna slipped from her car and crossed the street under cover of shadow. She edged along the building until she reached the same door they'd used.

It hadn't locked behind them.

Inside, the warehouse was dark, but her eyes adjusted quickly. She followed the echoes. A faint shuffling. The soft clink of metal.

Then a whisper.

"Sienna."

She turned.

Kai stood near a cage, holding a bolt cutter in one hand, a trembling dog leash in the other.

"What the hell are you doing?" she hissed.

He didn't flinch. "Saving them. What does it look like?"

"It looks like breaking and entering. Again. And obstruction. And interfering in an open investigation."

He nodded toward the cages. "They were going to kill the weak ones. Tonight."

"And what, you were going to just walk them out the front door?"

"If I had to."

Sienna exhaled hard. "Dammit, Kai."

"You going to arrest me?"

She didn't answer. She crouched beside the Lab and clipped on the leash.

"Let's move. Before they come back."

Kai

They cleared the warehouse in under five minutes.

Sienna backed her car into the alley while Kai carried the animals out two at a time—quiet, careful, methodical. The cats went into the cardboard carriers he kept folded in his satchel. The ferret curled into his hoodie pocket. The dogs rode low in the back seat, tails silent, eyes wide.

When they were done, Kai closed the car door gently and looked at her.

"You didn't have to help."

She slid into the driver's seat. "Yes, I did."

She didn't say why.

He didn't ask.

Sienna

They drove in silence for several blocks, past midnight diners and shuttered gas stations. The dog in the back whined softly, and Kai reached back without looking to rest a hand on her head.

"You're losing control of this," she said finally.

"I never had control," he said. "Only momentum."

She glanced at him. The circles under his eyes looked deeper than before. His hands trembled slightly—adrenaline, maybe. Or burnout.

"You can't keep going like this."

"I don't have a choice."

"You do. But you don't trust anyone else to make it."

He didn't respond.

They pulled up to the back entrance of the rescue clinic Sienna had used once before—unofficially, late at night, no questions asked. She knocked twice. A moment later, the door opened.

A tired vet tech took one look at the animals and nodded them inside.

Sienna helped unload.

Kai didn't follow.

When she came back out, he was already gone.

Here is **Chapter 19**, full-length and continuous in tone, voice, and pacing with the surrounding chapters:

Chapter 19
Consequences
Sienna

By the time she got back to her apartment, the adrenaline had worn off and the questions started.

How long could she keep doing this?

Covering for Kai. Skirting policy. Lying to her own department—by omission, if nothing else. All of it weighed heavier than the badge clipped to her belt.

She dropped her keys on the counter, peeled off her jacket, and sank into the couch. The silence wrapped around her like gauze—too quiet, too clean. The dog they'd rescued—Lyla, the vet tech had said—had licked her hand before they carried her into the clinic.

It was worth it.

It had to be worth it.

Her phone buzzed. A text from Cole.

You up?

She debated ignoring it. Then sighed and replied.

Barely.

A few seconds later:

Can I come by? We need to talk.

Sienna stared at the screen.
Not *want* to talk. *Need.*

Door's unlocked.

Cole

He arrived ten minutes later, still in uniform, his tie loosened, coat wet from the drizzle outside.

Sienna opened the door wider, gestured him in.

"You look like hell," he said.

"You should see the other guy," she replied, and shut the door behind him.

They sat in silence for a beat. Cole didn't waste time.

"There was a call over dispatch tonight. Warehouse break-in. South Docks. Anonymous tip said there were animals inside— injured ones. By the time animal control got there, the place was empty."

Sienna kept her face blank. "We're not assigned to that."

"No, we're not." He leaned forward. "But it was your signature, Sienna. Quiet entry. No damage. No witnesses. A clean sweep. If I didn't know better, I'd say it had Ghost written all over it."

She met his eyes. "Then maybe you know better."

He hesitated. "Do I?"

She didn't answer.

Cole sat back, jaw tightening. "I defended you, you know. When Internal was sniffing around after the Grayson case. I said you were principled. That you bent the rules, yeah, but always for the right reasons. But if you're still working with him..."

"I'm not," she said. A beat. Then softer: "Not officially."

"Jesus, Sienna."

"There were animals in that warehouse. Scheduled for transport —or worse. What was I supposed to do? Let them die while we waited for a warrant that might never come?"

He stood, pacing now. "You're a cop. You're supposed to trust the process."

"I *trusted* the process. For two years. It protected Grayson. It buried complaints. It made me complicit."

"That's not what this is anymore."

"Isn't it?"

He stared at her.

Finally, he sat again. "Okay. So what now? You going full vigilante again? Trade in your badge for a lockpick set?"

"I'm trying to do both," she said. "And it's tearing me apart."

Cole was quiet for a long time. Then: "You need to decide who you are, Sienna. Because if this keeps up, one of two things will happen: the department will catch you. Or the Ghost will drag you down with him."

Sienna rubbed her face. "He's not who he was before. He's trying. Working through the right channels when he can."

"Doesn't matter. The department doesn't care about intent. They care about liability. Optics. Chain of command."

She nodded. "I know."

"You want to help animals? Fine. You want to support better laws, more oversight? Great. But if you keep dancing between both worlds, you're going to fall."

He got up.

"Cole—"

He turned at the door. "I'm still in your corner. But I need you to give me a reason to stay there."

He left.

Sienna stood in the dark for a long time before she finally moved.

. . .

Kai

He didn't sleep.

Instead, he sat in the dark, staring at his wall of case notes and maps. Red string. Pins. Printed photos. Some things never changed.

But others had.

The last rescue hadn't gone clean. He'd made noise. Been seen. And Sienna... she'd looked at him differently tonight.

Less like a partner. More like a liability.

He couldn't blame her.

He was slipping.

The signals were coming more often now—stronger. Wider range. More pressure. Every time he tried to rest, another wave of panic, of pain, would crash over him. He couldn't tune it out anymore.

He didn't want to.

But he couldn't keep going like this, either.

He looked down at the photo he'd been holding.

A golden retriever. Bones showing through its fur. Nose pressed to the bars of a rusted crate.

Rescued. Safe now.

Worth it.

He set the photo down and reached for his burner phone.

He typed a message to Sienna.

I'm sorry. For dragging you in again. You don't have to keep covering for me. I'll figure it out another way.

He hit send.

And then, for the first time in weeks, he shut his eyes.

Sienna

The text came through just after dawn.

She read it twice, sitting on her front steps with a coffee she hadn't touched.

She didn't reply.

Not yet.

Instead, she stared at the rising sun over the rooftops, the edge of the city waking up.

And she wondered, again, what kind of cop she really was.

What kind of person she was trying to be.

Chapter 20
The Line
Kai

Kai stood at the edge of the rooftop, staring down at the alley below. The city felt quieter tonight—muted, still—but the pulse inside him didn't match. It throbbed like a migraine, raw and insistent.

He hadn't slept. Couldn't. Not after what had happened.

The rescue had gone sideways. The animals were safe, but Sienna had nearly been caught. He'd watched her sprint across a rooftop with sirens echoing and searchlights sweeping the skyline. And he'd caused it. Dragged her into this mess.

And now she was paying for it.

He'd felt the shift in her energy as soon as she got home last night. The tension. The guilt. The walls going up. The look she gave him before turning away.

He hadn't followed her.

He was beginning to realize that maybe he shouldn't have followed her in the first place.

Kai pulled out his phone. No new messages. No texts. He scrolled to her name, hovered his thumb over the call button.

Then locked the screen.

She needed space. And he needed to figure out who he was without dragging everyone down with him.

He turned away from the edge and headed back inside.

Sienna

Sienna sat in her car outside the precinct, hands gripping the steering wheel. She hadn't slept either. Not really. Every time she closed her eyes, she saw the lights, the sirens, the squad car skidding into the alley.

And Kai's face—part relief, part regret—just before he vanished again.

She hadn't told Cole everything. Not yet. But he knew enough. Knew she was lying. Knew she was hiding something.

And he was right.

She was hiding the fact that she believed in Kai more than she believed in the system she worked for.

Her phone buzzed. A text from Internal Affairs: *Reminder: Statement due by 4 PM regarding incident #004783.*

Right. The warehouse raid. The anonymous tip. The fact that she'd been just a little too close, a little too prepared.

She leaned her head back against the seat, eyes closed.

She was burning through favors. Stretching every inch of plausible deniability. And she was running out of room.

Her phone buzzed again. This time, a different message.

From Kai.

You okay?

She stared at the screen for a long time before typing back.

I don't know.

Cole

Cole paced in the precinct locker room, jaw tight. He'd seen the report. Knew the timelines didn't add up. Sienna had been on scene too fast. Had known too much. And she wasn't talking.

He wasn't sure what hurt more—that she was hiding something, or that she didn't trust him enough to tell him.

He remembered what Ortiz had said: *"She's been different lately."*

And now he was seeing it too.

Cole pulled out his phone, flipped through old texts from Sienna. Jokes. Case updates. Inside references. They hadn't just been partners—they'd been a team.

Now?

Now she was slipping away. And he didn't know why.

But he intended to find out.

Kai

Kai sat in the dim light of his apartment, scanning maps. Building layouts. Complaint records. He needed to stay focused. Keep moving. Keep helping.

But every time he looked at the screen, his vision blurred. His thoughts slid sideways.

The signals were worse lately—louder, messier. He couldn't always tell which ones were real and which were echoes. Couldn't always distinguish between pain he was sensing and pain he was feeling.

And then there was Sienna.

He'd told her he'd step back. That he didn't want to pull her down with him.

But the truth was, he didn't want to do this without her.

He was starting to lose the line. Between right and wrong. Between justice and obsession. Between who he was and what the Ghost had turned him into.

And she was the only thing tethering him to something human.

Sienna

By the time Sienna finished her shift, the sky was dark again. She drove aimlessly for a while, city lights blurring past her windows.

She ended up at a familiar corner. Parked. Walked.

Climbed a fire escape.

Kai's building.

She found him on the roof, sitting cross-legged, hoodie pulled up against the wind. He didn't turn when she approached.

"Hey," she said.

"Hey."

They sat in silence for a while, the city humming below.

Finally, Kai spoke. "I shouldn't have let you come on that rescue."

"You didn't let me. I chose to."

"I'm serious. It's getting dangerous. For you. And I can't keep asking you to—"

"You didn't ask," she said. "I offered."

Another pause. The wind tugged at her jacket.

"I almost lost my badge last night," she said. "Cole knows something's up. And IA's watching me."

"I know."

"I'm not saying that to guilt you. Just... to be clear about what this is."

Kai finally turned to look at her. "I never wanted you to get hurt."

"I know."

They sat in silence again.

"I've been thinking," Sienna said. "About the line."

"What line?"

"The one we keep crossing. The one between right and legal. Between justice and law."

Kai didn't respond.

DuMoire

"I don't know where it is anymore," she said. "But I think...
maybe the problem isn't that we're crossing it. Maybe it's that the line
was never where we thought it was in the first place."

He looked at her. Really looked at her.

And for a moment, the noise inside him quieted.

Chapter 21
The Legal Noose Tightens

S ienna sat in the City Hall conference room, surrounded by lawyers, politicians, and department brass. The air was thick with tension.

Captain Ortiz was beside her, arms crossed, jaw clenched. Across the table sat ADA Lee and two assistant DAs. At the head was Deputy Mayor Chen. On the screen, Grayson's lead attorney, Marcus Whitfield, stared out at them—flawless suit, perfect hair, the kind of man who won cases by outlasting you in paperwork and stamina.

"Let me be clear," Whitfield said, voice smooth and controlled. "My client, Leonard Grayson, is a respected member of this community. A city councilman. A philanthropist. And he has been the victim of an illegal police raid."

Sienna's jaw tightened. *Victim.*

"The raid was conducted without a warrant," he continued. "Without proper authorization. And without regard for my client's constitutional rights. Accordingly, we are filing an injunction to render all collected evidence inadmissible. We're also pursuing civil damages: unlawful entry, defamation, destruction of property."

Deputy Mayor Chen leaned in. "Mr. Whitfield, the animals on your client's property were in deplorable condition. Are you seriously denying that?"

"I'm not denying the condition of the animals. I'm stating, clearly, that the evidence was gathered illegally. And without admissible evidence, you have no case. Furthermore, my client maintains the animals were temporarily housed as part of a legitimate rescue partnership."

Sienna couldn't keep silent. "That's a lie. The dogs were neglected, overcrowded, malnourished. We have witness statements. We have—"

"Evidence obtained illegally," Whitfield cut in. "Which makes it worthless in court. Detective Halbrook, I don't doubt your passion. But the law is the law. And you broke it."

"I broke it to save lives."

"And in doing so, you handed my client a lawsuit that could cost this city millions. And you've destroyed your own career."

"Enough," Deputy Mayor Chen said, holding up a hand. "Mr. Whitfield, we understand your position. But let's be clear: your client's property was the site of serious animal cruelty. The public won't forget that."

"The public will forget what the media tells them to forget. And right now, the media's focused on the Ghost Rescuer—a vigilante who broke into my client's property and caused substantial damage. That is the story. Not my client's supposed crimes."

He ended the call. The screen went dark.

Silence hung over the room.

Then Chen turned to Ortiz. "Captain, catch the Ghost. Not next week. Now. The only way out of this is shifting public focus onto the vigilante. If we can't, the department takes the fall."

Ortiz nodded once. "Understood."

Chen turned to Sienna. "Detective Halbrook. You're suspended, but let's be blunt: you've put this department in an impossible position. Unless we catch the Ghost—and soon—you'll be the scapegoat. Grayson's lawyers will see to that."

Sienna's gut twisted. "I acted in good faith. I was trying to save lives."

"I believe that. But courtrooms don't care about belief. They care about proof. And right now, all the proof says you broke the law."

"So what do you want from me?"

"I want you to help us catch the Ghost. Quietly. Off the record. And when we do, you testify that you were trying to stop him, not help him."

Sienna stared at her. "You want me to lie."

"I want you to survive. Because if you don't, you lose your badge, your pension, your career. Everything."

By the time she returned to the precinct, Sienna was shaking—not from fear, but fury.

Grayson was walking. And now she was the one on trial. For doing the right thing.

She stormed into the war room. Tommy looked up from his workstation and immediately stood.

"What happened?"

"Grayson's lawyers filed an injunction. All evidence from the raid is inadmissible. They're suing the department. And Chen wants me to help catch Kai—off the record—so they can shift the blame."

Tommy winced. "Jesus. Are you going to do it?"

Sienna stared at the whiteboard, covered in maps, case notes, timelines.

"I don't know. Part of me thinks I should. Kai's making it worse. He's giving Grayson's lawyers fuel."

"And the other part?"

"The other part thinks he's right. That the system is broken. And catching him would be a betrayal of everything I believe in."

Tommy was quiet a moment. "So... what are you going to do?"

"I'm going to meet him. Noon. Coffee shop on Fifth. Like we agreed."

"You're still doing that? After what Chen just said?"

"I'm not bringing him in. I'm going to talk to him. See if there's a way to work together instead of against each other."

"That's a hell of a gamble."

"I know. But it's the only play I've got."

11:47 a.m. — Kai

Kai sat in the corner booth, eyes on the door. He'd arrived early, scouted exits, mapped cameras—old habits. The place was busy: students, laptop workers, lunch-break suits. No one looked twice at him.

11:48. Almost time.

He half-expected this to be a trap. Sienna with backup. Handcuffs.

But she'd let him go before. Maybe she really did want to talk.

At 11:52, she walked in. Jeans, jacket, no badge, no gun. She scanned the room, saw him, and came over.

"You came," she said.

"So did you."

She slid into the booth. "I wasn't sure you would."

"I wasn't sure you'd come alone."

"I did. This is just us."

He studied her. She looked tired. Worn thin. Like someone still fighting even though she knew she was losing.

"You look like hell," he said.

"Thanks. You too."

Kai almost smiled.

A waitress came by. "Can I get you anything?"

"Coffee, black," they both said.

When she left, Sienna leaned in.

"Grayson's lawyers filed an injunction. All the evidence from the raid is out. He's going to walk."

Kai's jaw clenched. "So the system failed. Again."

"It did. And now they're blaming me. And you. Chen wants me to catch you so they can hang this whole thing around your neck and save face."

"Are you going to?"

"No. But I need your help."

He frowned. "With what?"

"Building a case. A real one. That can actually stick."

"You think that's possible?"

"I don't know. But if we keep going like this, we both lose. You get arrested. I lose my badge. And Grayson walks."

The waitress dropped off their coffees. Bitter. Strong.

Kai stirred his with a spoon, eyes never leaving Sienna. "What do you need?"

"Everything you've got. Locations. Property records. Financials. Anything I can use legally."

"And in return?"

"I'll do everything I can to keep you out of jail. No promises. But I'll try."

Kai was quiet. He'd worked alone for so long. Trusted no one. But maybe Sienna was different.

"I've got records. Public data. No hacking. Just a lot of digging. You can use it."

Sienna blinked. "You've already built the case."

"I had to. I needed to know where the animals were."

"Will you share it?"

He hesitated, then nodded. "Yeah. But I'm not stopping."

"I'm not asking you to. I'm asking you to be smarter. To work with me."

"And if the system fails again?"

"Then we figure something else out. Together."

He studied her a long moment.

"You're not asking me to trust the system."

"No. I'm asking you to trust me."

Kai pulled out his phone, opened a folder, and slid it across the table.

"Shell companies. Complaint logs. Properties. It's all there."

Sienna scrolled. Her eyes widened.

"This is... good."

"I'm thorough."

She looked up at him. "Thank you."

"Don't thank me yet. We've still got to take him down."

"We will," she said. "Together."

2:15 p.m. — Sienna

Back in her apartment, Sienna spread Kai's files across her table. The pattern was there—money funneled through fake companies, properties listed under ghost names, complaints buried in bureaucracy.

It was a start.

Her phone buzzed. A text from Tommy:

Got something. East side property. Shell company. Multiple complaints. No follow-up.

Her pulse jumped.

Send me the address.

Thirty seconds later:

Already did. Be careful.

By 10 p.m., Sienna was parked a block from the building. Dark. Fenced. Another warehouse. Another cage.

She walked the perimeter, staying out of sight. No warrant. No backup. Just observation.

She heard barking. Faint. But real.

Her jaw clenched.

She raised her phone, took photos of the structure, the lot, the security gaps.

Then she called Tommy.

"I need you to file a complaint with animal control. Anonymous. Use this address. Flag it urgent."

"You sure?"

"This time, we do it right. No shortcuts."

"Got it."

She hung up. Listened.

The barking continued.

She turned and walked away.

Not because she wanted to.

Because it was the only way to win.

Chapter 22
Slipping Patterns

K ai stood on the rooftop, staring at the city, trying to ignore the feeling that he was being watched.

It had started three days ago. A patrol car idling on his street—engine running, lights off, just sitting there for twenty minutes before pulling away. A helicopter overhead, its spotlight sweeping rooftops. More police in the industrial zones, the parking garages, the places he usually operated.

At first, he'd told himself it was coincidence. Routine. But it wasn't.

They were looking for him. Systematically. Predicting his movements. Closing the net.

And they were getting closer.

He pulled out his phone, opened the scanner app. Police chatter had spiked—more units on animal-related calls, more sweeps in Ghost-active zones.

Sienna was tightening the net.

He closed the app. He could disappear for a while. Lay low. Wait for it to blow over.

But the signals were still coming—fear, hunger, despair.

He couldn't stop.

Not yet.

Even if it meant getting caught.

That night, he drove east, chasing a weak but steady signal: a dog, trapped in a storage unit, abandoned after an eviction. Fear. Hunger. Fading fast.

Kai parked two blocks away, grabbed his tools, and walked. Industrial streets. Chain-link fences. Sodium lights turned everything amber and black.

The storage facility was fenced, the gate padlocked. Cameras scanned the entrance, but he'd mapped their blind spots.

He slipped through the perimeter, moving like smoke.

Unit 47. The signal came from the back. The lock was heavy-duty, weatherproof, solid steel.

He crouched, pulled out his picks, and went to work.

Click.

Click.

Another pin.

Then—a low rumble.

A car.

Headlights flashed across the fence.

Patrol.

Too early.

He worked faster, sweat on his brow, hands trembling.

Click.

Click.

The lock gave.

He yanked it off, pulled open the door.

A small terrier mix crouched against the wall, filthy and shaking.

"Come on," he whispered. "No time."

The dog hesitated—then limped forward.

Kai scooped it up, tucked it into his jacket, and ran.

Behind him, the patrol car entered the lot. A spotlight swept the rows.

He slipped through the fence, sprinted down the alley. His lungs burned. The dog whimpered, burrowed deeper.

"You're safe now," Kai whispered.

At the car, he yanked open the door, placed the dog on the passenger seat, and peeled away into the night.

But as the city blurred past his windows, a thought dropped into his gut like a stone.

His tools.

He'd left one behind.

Two blocks away, he pulled over and searched his pockets.

Lock picks. Flashlight. Gloves.

No tension wrench.

The specialized one Eli had given him. With the shop logo engraved on the handle.

Evidence.

Traceable.

His stomach dropped.

He could go back. Try to retrieve it. But the patrol was still there.

And Sienna? She'd find it. She'd know exactly what it was.

He stared at the wheel.

The dog was safe.

That had to be enough.

He drove.

The next morning, Kai sat in Eli's shop, trying to explain.

Eli listened, face darkening.

"You dropped the wrench?"

"Yeah."

"The one with my shop's name on it?"

Kai nodded.

Eli stood, rubbed his eyes. "Do you get what that means? If they find it, it leads to me. They'll ask questions I can't answer without lying. Or implicating you."

"I know. I'm sorry."

"Sorry doesn't fix it."

"I had to act. The dog—"

"And now you're going to get caught. And you're dragging me with you."

Kai's frustration flared. "So what? I should've left the dog to die?"

"I want you to think before you act. To stop making mistakes that will ruin you."

"I'm trying."

Eli shook his head. "Not hard enough. I care about you, Kai. But I can't protect you anymore. If the police come, I tell the truth. I won't lie. I won't risk my business, my freedom, for this."

Kai stood, jacket in hand. "You're cutting me loose."

"I'm protecting myself. Because you won't."

Kai hesitated at the door. "I'm sorry. For dragging you in. For everything."

Eli didn't respond.

Kai walked out. Didn't look back.

That afternoon, he sat in his apartment, staring at the wall.

Eli was right.

He was slipping.

Leaving evidence. Making noise. Taking risks.

And the net was closing.

His phone buzzed.

A number he didn't recognize.

I found your tool. We need to talk.

His heart skipped.

Sienna.

He typed a single word:

Where?

The reply came quickly:

Brennan's. One hour.

Kai pocketed the phone and left.

Brennan's was dark. Closed for the day.

Sienna stood outside, arms folded.

Kai approached slowly. "You found it."

She held up a plastic evidence bag. The wrench inside gleamed under the streetlight.

"Dropped it at the storage unit," she said. "Has your prints. Eli's logo. Everything I need to arrest you."

"But you haven't."

"No."

"Why?"

"Because I don't want to. Because arresting you won't stop Grayson. And because I think you're doing the right thing—even if the method's wrong."

Kai's eyes narrowed. "So what do you want?"

"I want you to stop. To stop taking dumb risks. Stop leaving evidence."

"I can't. Not while the signals are still coming in."

"Then work with me. Give me what I need to build the case legally. I'll do everything I can to keep you out of jail."

"You're asking me to trust you again."

"Yeah. I am."

"Why should I?"

"Because we're running out of time. And if someone else catches you, I won't be able to protect you."

Kai was silent a long moment.

"What do you need?"

"I need you to stop making mistakes. And let me handle Grayson."

"And if that doesn't work?"

"Then we figure it out. Together."

He searched her face. She was tired. Committed. And deeply conflicted.

"Fine," he said. "I'll work with you. But I'm not stopping. Not until he's held accountable."

"I can live with that."

She pocketed the wrench and walked away.

Kai stayed, watching her go. Then he pulled out his phone and checked the scanner.

More patrols. More units. More surveillance.

The net was closing.

That night, Kai stood on the rooftop, the city alive beneath him.

He'd been a ghost. Careful. Invisible.

Not anymore.

The police knew who he was.

They were closing in.

He thought about the wrench. Sienna's choice not to use it.

She believed in him. Or wanted to.

But how long would that last?

How long before she had to choose between justice and the job?

He didn't know.

But the signals hadn't stopped.

And neither could he.

Even if it meant getting caught.

Even if it meant losing everything.

DuMoire

Because doing nothing was worse.
He stepped closer to the edge, the wind lifting his jacket.
The city pulsed below—light and noise and suffering.
He used to move in the shadows.
But the light was chasing him now.
And he didn't know how much longer he could run.

Chapter 23
Pressure Breaks Lines

S ienna sat in her car in the precinct parking lot, engine off, staring at the dashboard. It was past 10 p.m. The lot was mostly empty. The building behind her glowed softly in the dark, but she couldn't bring herself to go inside.

She'd been suspended for three days. Officially, she wasn't supposed to be here. Not supposed to be working the case.

But Tommy had let her in through the back. Given her access. Helped her track Kai's movements, map Grayson's holdings, build what the department had refused to.

Now she sat alone, trying to figure out what came next.

Her phone buzzed. A text from Cole.

Where are you?

Sienna hesitated, then typed:

Parking lot. Thinking.

Thirty seconds later:

Meet me at Brennan's. We need to talk.

She stared at the message.

Brennan's. The bar two blocks from the precinct. Where cops went when things couldn't be said on the record.

She started the engine and drove.

Brennan's smelled like old beer and older grease. The lighting was dim, the floors sticky, the regulars quiet.

Cole was in a booth near the window, nursing a beer. He looked tired.

Sienna slid into the seat across from him. "What's going on?"

He took a sip, then set the glass down. "Ortiz called me in. Asked about you. What you've been doing."

Her stomach tightened. "What'd you tell him?"

"I said you were laying low. He didn't buy it. He knows you're still working the case. And he's pissed."

"I'm trying to catch the Ghost. Isn't that what he wants?"

"He wants you to follow orders. You're suspended, Sienna. You're working off the books. Using Tommy's access. If this blows up, they'll pin it all on you."

She leaned back. "So what should I do? Walk away? Let Grayson keep operating?"

"I want you to be smart. Think about your career. Right now, you're on thin ice."

"I don't care about my career. I care about doing the right thing."

Cole looked at her. "That's dangerous thinking."

"Because it doesn't protect Ortiz's budget? Or Lee's conviction rate?"

"No. Because it gets people fired. Or worse." He leaned in. "You're starting to sound like the Ghost. That scares me."

Her frustration sparked. "The Ghost is exposing the system's failure. Doing what we should have done. And we're hunting him for it."

"He's a vigilante. He's breaking the law. He's inspiring copycats who don't know what they're doing."

"So is ignoring people like Grayson. Letting him operate unchecked. Ignoring complaints while animals suffer."

Cole's voice softened. "You don't think the Ghost is dangerous."

"I think he's trying to do the right thing. Like me."

"That's what I'm afraid of."

They sat in silence, the low buzz of the bar around them.

"I'm not aligned with the department anymore," she said quietly. "I don't trust Ortiz. Or Lee. Or the system. Not after this."

"So what now?"

"I find the Ghost before anyone else does. And I find a way to stop Grayson without destroying Kai in the process."

"And if you can't?"

"Then I'll make a choice. My choice. No one else's."

He studied her. "You're crossing a line."

"I know."

"And you're okay with that?"

"I don't know. But I know I can't keep doing it the old way. Something has to change."

He nodded. "Be careful. If this goes sideways, I can't protect you. No one can."

"I know."

Past midnight, Sienna dropped onto her couch, exhausted. Cole was right. She was crossing lines. Aligning with a vigilante. Disobeying orders. Operating outside the law.

But the system had failed. And she was done waiting for it to fix itself.

She opened her thread with Kai. His last message still sat there:

I'll work with you. But I'm not stopping. Not until Grayson's held accountable.

She pulled up the financial records. The shell companies. The money trails. The pieces were there. A case was forming.

She started typing—drafting a report, documenting irregularities, building something that didn't rely on the raid or inadmissible evidence.

By 3 a.m., she was done.

She sent the file to Tommy.

Can you verify these records? I need to know if they're solid.

Then she tried to sleep.

But all she could think about was Kai—the man she was supposed to arrest, and the one she now understood better than anyone.

The next morning, Sienna sat in a coffee shop across from Brennan's Restoration Shop, watching the entrance. Waiting.

Her phone buzzed. A text from Tommy.

Records check out. Grayson's laundering money through shells. Possibly tax evasion. Enough for an investigation.

Her pulse quickened.

Can you forward it to the FBI? Financial crimes?

Already did. They're interested. But it'll take time. Weeks, maybe months.

She stared at the screen. Weeks. Months. While animals kept suffering.

And Kai? He wouldn't wait.

She typed a message:

Where are you? We need to talk.

No response.

Five minutes. Ten.

She stood, crossed the street, and entered the shop.

Eli was behind the counter with a newspaper. He looked up.

"Detective Halbrook. Thought you were suspended."

"I am. Still working. Is Kai here?"

He hesitated. Then shook his head. "Not in two days."

"Do you know where he went?"

"No. And if I did, I don't know if I'd tell you."

She leaned on the counter. "I'm not here to arrest him. I'm here to help. But I can't if I can't find him."

Eli studied her. "You're not like the others."

"No. I'm not."

"You think he's doing the right thing."

"I think he's trying to. But he's going to get himself killed if he keeps this up. I don't want that on my conscience."

Eli sighed. "He's at a warehouse. East side, near the old rail yard. Only standing building in the area. Can't miss it."

"Thank you."

"For what it's worth, I hope you stop him. Before it's too late. I care about that kid. I don't want to see him throw his life away."

She nodded and left.

The warehouse was just as described. Three stories. Broken windows. Graffiti. Surrounded by rusted rails and dead lots.

She parked a block away, walked to the side entrance, and stepped inside.

"Kai?" she called. "It's Sienna. I'm not here to arrest you."

Silence.

"I know you're here. Eli told me. I'm trying to help."

Still nothing.

She climbed to the second floor. Found a makeshift living space—sleeping bag, tools, supplies. But no Kai.

She texted him:

I'm at the warehouse. Where are you?

Thirty seconds later:

I'm not there. And I'm not coming back. It's not safe anymore.

She stared at the reply.

Not safe.

Because they were closing in.

Then where are you? I have info on Grayson. We can use it.

Another pause. Then:

Old train station. Midnight. Come alone.

She pocketed the phone, looked around the empty space. Kai was isolated. Cornered.

And now, they'd meet—one more time. To decide what came next.

That night, she sat at her kitchen table, the case files spread like a battlefield.

Financial records. Property deeds. Complaint logs.

She had everything—except time.

Kai wouldn't wait. And neither could she.

She looked at his text again:

Old train station. Midnight. Come alone.

It was reckless. Unauthorized. Possibly dangerous.

But Sienna was done waiting. Done playing by the rules.

She grabbed her jacket and walked out.

The train station was abandoned. Forgotten. Perfect.

Or fatal.

She didn't know which.

She didn't know how to win. But she knew she couldn't quit.

The fight wasn't over.

And neither was she.

Chapter 24
Media Crossfire

Mina sat in the green room at Channel 7, staring at her phone, trying to calm her nerves. She'd been invited onto *City Pulse*, a local talk show covering politics, crime, and social issues. Tonight's topic: the Ghost Rescuer.

She'd covered the Ghost for months. But this—live television—was different. Her face, her voice, her words, broadcast to thousands.

She wasn't sure she was ready.

Raj, her editor, had insisted. *"This is your story, Mina. You broke it. You built it. Now you need to own it."*

But after Marcus Martinez... after realizing her words had consequences she couldn't control... she wasn't sure she *wanted* to.

A production assistant poked her head in. "Five minutes, Ms. Torres."

Mina nodded, pocketed her phone, and stood. Checked her reflection—blazer, minimal makeup, hair pulled back. Professional. Composed.

Even if she didn't feel it.

.   .   .

162

The studio was smaller than she expected. A circular table with four chairs. Cameras. Bright lights.

The host, Danielle Park, was already seated. Two other guests were being mic'd—Claudia Reyes, director of the local animal rights coalition, and Officer Marcus Lin, a police spokesperson.

Mina took her seat and tried to breathe.

Danielle opened the show. "The Ghost Rescuer. A vigilante breaking into cars and properties to free animals in distress. Some call him a hero. Others, a criminal. Tonight, we explore what his actions mean for our city."

She turned to Claudia. "Ms. Reyes, you've been vocal in your support. Why?"

Claudia leaned forward, firm. "Because he's doing what the system won't. Animals suffer in this city every day—locked in hot cars, trapped in breeding operations—and the system is too slow, too underfunded, too indifferent to respond. The Ghost fills that gap."

Officer Lin shook his head. "With respect, the Ghost is breaking the law. Trespassing. Damaging property. Inspiring copycats. One teenager's already been arrested trying to imitate him. Vigilantism is dangerous."

"What's dangerous," Claudia countered, "is doing nothing. The Ghost has saved over forty animals in six months. How many has the department saved?"

"We respond to every call. But we can't be everywhere. And we can't break the law to enforce it."

"Then maybe the law needs to change."

Danielle turned to Mina. "Ms. Torres, you've followed this story from the beginning. Hero or criminal?"

All eyes turned. Lights. Cameras. Pressure.

Mina took a breath. "I think he's both. He's doing something necessary—but he's also outside the law. The real question isn't whether he's a hero or a criminal. It's: *Why does he exist?* What does it say about our city that someone felt compelled to act this way?"

Danielle nodded. "You've written about the systemic failures that created him. Do those failures justify his actions?"

"They explain them. Justification? That's something everyone has to decide for themselves."

"Do you have sources close to the Ghost?" Danielle asked. "Do you know who he is?"

Mina's pulse jumped. *There it is.*

"I don't know who he is," she said carefully. "And even if I did, I wouldn't reveal that. My job is to report facts—not expose sources."

"But your articles have included details only the Ghost would know."

"I've received anonymous tips. But I've never met the Ghost. And I've never confirmed his identity."

It was a lie. Or at least, a half-truth.

Danielle turned to Lin. "Officer, is the investigation making progress?"

Lin kept his tone neutral. "We're following leads. We're confident we'll identify the suspect soon."

Claudia jumped in. "What about Leonard Grayson? His property was raided. Are you investigating him?"

A beat.

"Mr. Grayson's property was the site of an unauthorized entry. That's under review. But he hasn't been charged."

"Because the evidence was obtained illegally," Claudia said. "But the animals were real. The suffering was real. And Grayson's lawyers are using technicalities to avoid accountability."

Lin didn't flinch. "The law is the law. We can't pick and choose."

"Then maybe *that's* the problem."

Danielle turned back to Mina. "You've written about Grayson's political connections. Do you think they're protecting him?"

Mina paused. "Grayson is a powerful man with powerful friends.

And that power has insulated him. Complaints were filed. Nothing was done. The pattern is clear."

"Do you think the Ghost targeted him specifically?"

"I think the Ghost responds to suffering. And Grayson's property was full of it."

Danielle nodded. "We'll be right back after this break."

The lights dimmed. Cameras stopped rolling. Mina finally exhaled.

Claudia leaned in. "You handled that well. But you're holding back. You know more than you're saying."

Mina didn't answer.

After the show, Mina sat in her car in the studio lot, staring at her phone.

She hadn't exposed Kai. Hadn't revealed her sources.

But she'd lied.

A text from Raj lit the screen.

Great job. Interview's already trending. Keep it up.

She set the phone down.

Trending.

Her phone buzzed again. Unknown number.

Thank you for not revealing my identity. I know it wasn't easy.

Kai.

He'd been watching.

She typed:

I'm a journalist, not a cop. But are you going after Grayson again?

Thirty seconds later:

I have to. He's still hurting animals. And the system won't stop him.

She clenched the phone.

If you try again, you'll get caught. Or worse. Let the system work.

Pause.

The system doesn't work. You know that. You've written about it.

Her own words, turned back on her.

I'm not saying the system's perfect. But vigilantism isn't the answer.

Quick reply:

Better than doing nothing.

Mina leaned back. He wasn't going to stop. Not for her. Not for anyone.

And she'd helped make him. Built the story. Gave him a voice. A myth.

And now she might have to be the one to stop him.

The next morning, Mina sat at her desk, laptop open. The interview had sparked debate. But she didn't care about discourse anymore.

She cared about truth.

She opened a new document:

Working Title: The Ghost Unmasked

Angle: Investigative Profile

Sources: Anonymous tips, police contacts, locksmiths, animal control

This wasn't myth-making. This was journalism. And it was dangerous.

If she exposed Kai, she'd betray a source.

If she didn't, she'd be complicit in whatever came next.

Her phone buzzed. Unknown number.

If you're serious about understanding the Ghost, meet me. Old train station. Midnight. Come alone.

Mina frowned. Not Kai. The tone was different.

Who is this?

Reply:

**Someone who knows the truth. And wants to help
you tell it.**

She stared at the message.

It was a risk.

But it might be the story.

That night, Mina sat in her car outside the old train station. Abandoned. Dark. Empty lots. Rusted rails.

11:58 p.m.

She grabbed her flashlight and stepped into the cold.

The station was bigger than she expected. Broken windows. Graffiti. Boarded doors.

One door was ajar.

She pushed it open.

"Hello?" she called. "I'm here. Where are you?"

No answer.

She moved deeper, light slicing through the dark.

"I got your message. I'm here to talk."

Still nothing.

Then—footsteps. Behind her.

She turned, flashlight up.

A figure emerged from the shadows. A woman. Jeans. Jacket.

Sienna Halbrook.

Mina blinked. "You sent the text."

Sienna nodded. "We need to talk. About the Ghost. About Grayson. About what comes next."

"Why me?"

"You're the only one he trusts. And if we don't stop him, he's going to get himself killed."

Mina lowered the flashlight. "What do you want from me?"

"Help me stop him. Before it's too late."

"And in exchange?"

"I'll give you the story. The real one. Who he is. Why he's doing this. What it means."

Mina stared at her. This was it. The chance to move past the myth. To get to the truth.

But it meant betraying Kai.

"I need to think."

"You don't have time. He's planning something big. And if we don't act—he'll be caught. Or worse."

Mina swallowed. "What's he planning?"

"I don't know. But it involves Grayson. And it's happening soon."

Trust Sienna? Work with her?

Or walk away?

"All right," Mina said. "I'll help. But I want the whole story. No secrets."

"Deal."

They stood in silence, two women on opposite sides of the system, caught in the storm they'd both helped create.

And the fight was only just beginning.

Chapter 25
The Trap

K ai stood in the shadows across from Riverside Park, watching the parking lot. It was past 11 p.m., the air cool and damp with the smell of cut grass and river water. The lot was mostly empty—just a few scattered cars. One of them, a silver SUV parked near the back, had been there for hours.

And inside, Kai could feel it. The pulse. Faint but steady.

A dog. Trapped. Suffering.

He'd been monitoring the scanner all evening. No calls. No dispatches. No response from animal control.

The system was ignoring it. Again.

Which meant the dog would suffer all night. Dehydration. Heat-stroke. Maybe worse.

Unless he acted.

He knew the pattern. Hot day. Irresponsible owner. Dog left in a car for hours. By the time someone called it in, it was usually too late.

But not this time.

Kai checked his phone—no patrols nearby, no surveillance signals. The park's old cameras covered the playground and main entrance, but the parking lot was a blind spot.

Perfect.

He grabbed his tools and crossed the street, moving low and fast. Silent footsteps. Controlled breathing. Every movement deliberate.

He'd done this dozens of times. He knew the routine. But something felt off tonight. The air too still. The silence too deep. And the pulse—the signal from the dog—felt almost too easy. Too staged.

He shook it off. Paranoia. The cops didn't know where he'd strike next. They couldn't.

Could they?

He reached the SUV and peered through the window. A beagle mix, curled in the back seat, panting hard. Tongue lolling. Eyes wide and glassy.

The windows were cracked maybe an inch. Not enough.

The pulse surged—fear, pain, desperation.

Kai slid the slim jim into the frame. Angle. Hook. Pull.

The lock popped with a quiet *click*.

He eased the door open. Heat blasted out like from an oven. The dog scrambled out, trembling and frantic, stumbling in its desperation to escape.

Kai crouched. "It's okay," he said gently. "You're safe now."

The dog hesitated, sniffed his hand, then licked it—tongue dry and rough.

He pulled out a water bottle, poured it into a collapsible bowl. The dog drank greedily, water splashing onto the asphalt.

Kai scanned the lot. Still quiet. Still dark.

Too quiet.

He felt it again—wrongness. Like he was being watched.

But the tree line was still. The street empty. No headlights. No sirens.

Just silence.

He pulled out a marker and scrawled on the windshield in bold black strokes:

DO MORE.

Then he locked the door, slid the slim jim back into his kit, and turned to go.

The dog followed a few steps, confused, water dripping from its muzzle.

Kai pointed toward the lit path at the park entrance. "Go. Find someone. You're okay now."

The dog hesitated, then trotted off, tail low but moving.

Kai slipped back into the shadows.

What he didn't see was the camera.

It wasn't one of the old park security models. This one was new—high-res, infrared, mounted high on a light pole with a clear view of the lot.

Tommy Chen had installed it two days ago, part of Sienna's sting.

They'd mapped Kai's pattern—foot traffic, complaints, lighting, proximity to shelters. Riverside Park had topped the list.

And the trap had worked.

The camera caught everything: Kai's approach, his face half-lit by the sodium glow, the tools, the careful entry. The message.

Everything Sienna needed to make the arrest.

In a surveillance van two blocks away, Tommy hunched over his laptop, watching the live feed. The infrared camera lit Kai's figure against the cooler dark.

"Got him," Tommy said softly.

Sienna leaned over his shoulder. She'd waited three hours in the van, hoping he'd take the bait.

The SUV had been planted at 8 p.m., rigged with a heat signature decoy that mimicked a distressed dog.

And now, here he was.

The footage was clear in all the right places. His face, visible in profile. The way he held the slim jim. The practiced movements. The marker across the windshield.

It was him. Kai DuMoire.

The Ghost.

"Rewind to 23:14," Sienna said. "When he looks up."

Tommy scrubbed back. Stopped on the frame.

Kai's face, caught in the streetlight, eyes searching. No idea he was staring straight into the lens.

"Freeze it."

Done.

Kai's face filled the screen. Young. Focused. Tired. Determined.

Not a criminal. Not a villain. Just a man trying to fix something broken.

And now she had to arrest him.

"Run facial recognition," she said.

Tommy typed. "This footage is solid, Sienna. Facial ID, tool usage, the signature tag—it's all here. We can get a warrant today."

Sienna didn't answer. She just watched the loop—Kai crouching, giving water. Writing *DO MORE* like a message to the world.

The dog hadn't been real. But Kai had believed it. He'd risked everything for it.

And that made this harder.

"Match confirmed," Tommy said. "Kai DuMoire. 94% confidence. No priors. Age 26. Clean record."

She closed her eyes. She'd known for weeks. But knowing wasn't the same as proving.

"Package the footage," she said finally. "Send it to Ortiz. Set a briefing for tomorrow."

"You sure?"

"No. But I don't have a choice."

Tommy hesitated. "We could... lose the footage. Say the equipment failed."

"To what end?" she said. "So he keeps pushing his luck until someone less careful catches him?"

No answer.

"I need to do this now," Sienna said. "On my terms. Because if I wait, someone else will take him down their way. And I can't protect him from that."

Tommy turned back to the laptop. "All right. Sending the package now. For what it's worth... I think he's doing good work."

"He is," she said. "That's why this hurts."

She stared at the screen a moment longer, then pulled out her phone.

Typed:

I know you were at Riverside Park. I have footage. We need to talk. Before this gets worse.

She hit send.

And sat in silence, watching the street outside.

Kai walked back to his apartment, the pulse fading. The rescue was done.

But the unease lingered.

He checked the scanner again. Still nothing. No dispatch. No calls.

Which was strange. Someone *always* called.

Unless there'd never been a dog.

The thought hit hard.

He sat on the futon, phone in hand, breath shallow.

His phone buzzed.

A text from an unknown number.

I know you were at Riverside Park. I have footage. We need to talk. Before this gets worse.

His chest tightened. He knew who it was.

Sienna.

She'd been there. She'd watched. She had proof.

His hands shook as he typed:

What do you want?

The reply came quickly.

I want you to stop. Before you get yourself killed. Meet me. Tomorrow night. Old train station. We'll figure this out together.

Kai stared at the message.

Together. Like there was a way through this that didn't end with handcuffs.

But she was a cop. And her job was clear.

He typed:

I'll think about it.

Then he set the phone down and lay back.

He *had* been watched. He *had* been set up. And he *had* made a mistake.

The net was closing.

He could run. Disappear. Start over.

But the signals would still be there. Animals suffering. Trapped. Forgotten.

Running wasn't the answer.

He had to finish this. Stop Grayson. Do what the system wouldn't.

Even if it meant getting caught.

Even if it meant losing everything.

Because doing nothing? That was worse.

The Red Light

High above the lot at Riverside Park, the camera's red light blinked steadily in the dark.

Watching.

Recording.

Waiting.

The trap had worked.

And the Ghost was running out of time.

Chapter 26
Burned Bridges

Kai stood outside Brennan's Restoration Shop, staring at the door. He'd been avoiding Eli for three days—ever since their last tense conversation. Ever since Eli made it clear he was uncomfortable with what Kai was doing.

But Kai needed tools. Specialty picks. Tension wrenches. The kind of equipment he couldn't get anywhere else. And Eli was the only one who could provide them.

The Night Before

Kai had spent the previous night pacing his apartment, Sienna's text burning in his mind:

I know you were at Riverside Park. I have footage. We need to talk. Before this gets worse.

Footage. Clear footage. His face, his tools, his technique. Everything she needed to arrest him.

He'd replayed the Riverside rescue in his head a dozen times, searching for the mistake. And he'd found it. That brief glance up while scanning the lot. Two seconds. Maybe three. His face lit by the sodium lights as he looked right at a camera he didn't know was there.

Two seconds. That's all it took.

Now, the clock was ticking. Sienna had proof. Which meant she could get a warrant. Which meant Kai had maybe forty-eight hours— if he was lucky.

If he was going to stop Grayson, he had to move fast. And for that, he needed Eli.

Swallowing his pride felt like choking. But the alternative was worse.

The bell chimed as Kai pushed open the shop door. Eli was at the counter, bent over a lock. He looked up, expression shifting—surprise, then wariness, then something harder.

"Kai."

"Eli."

They stared at each other, tension thick between them.

"I need tools," Kai said.

Eli set the lock down. Crossed his arms. "I told you. I'm not comfortable with this anymore."

"I know. But I'm asking anyway."

"Why? So you can keep taking risks? Keep leaving evidence? Keep making mistakes that'll get you arrested?"

"I'm being more careful now."

Eli's voice sharpened. "Are you? Because I've been watching the news. Reading Mina's pieces. The Ghost is all over the place. You're still out there, night after night, like you're invincible."

"I'm not. I know the risks."

"Then why keep going?"

"Because someone has to. Because the animals are still suffering. Because the system's still failing."

Eli shook his head. "You sound like your father."

Kai stiffened. "What's that supposed to mean?"

"He was passionate. Smart. But he was stubborn. Thought he could fix the world by himself. And it broke him. I watched it happen. And I don't want to watch it happen again."

"I'm not him."

"No," Eli said, voice grim. "You're worse. He knew his limits. You don't. You just keep pushing. And sooner or later, you're going to fall."

Kai's frustration rose. "So I should just walk away? Let Grayson keep hurting animals?"

"I want you to be smart. You're one person. You can't win this fight alone."

Kai's voice cracked. "Then help me."

Eli's voice softened—but didn't bend. "I can't. Not anymore. Helping you means putting myself at risk. I'm not willing to do that."

"So you're just giving up?"

"I'm being realistic. You break the law, you get caught. That's not justice. That's reckless."

"You're wrong."

"Am I? Look at yourself. You're exhausted. Isolated. You dropped a tool at a scene—with my shop's logo on it. If the cops trace it, I go down with you."

Kai froze.

"You didn't even notice, did you? That's how close you are to blowing this. And dragging me down with you."

"I didn't mean to—"

"But you did. That's the point. You're so deep in this, you can't see the fallout. Not for me, not for Sienna, not for Mina. You never asked for help—you just expected it."

Kai's voice was low. "Sixty animals. I've saved sixty lives. That's what's changed."

"And how many more are suffering right now? Hundreds? Thousands? You can't save them all."

"So I do nothing?"

"No. You accept your limits. You fight smart. You live to keep doing it."

Kai's voice hardened. "My father didn't accept his limits."

Eli's reply was quiet. "And he died alone. Burned out. Bitter. Is that what you want?"

"I want to make a difference."

"You already are. But you're burning your life to do it. And I won't be part of that. Not again."

Kai stared at him, jaw clenched.

"Then fine. I'll do it without you. I don't need your tools. I don't need anything from you."

"Kai—"

"You made your choice. I've made mine. You want to sit back and let the world stay broken? Go ahead. But don't expect me to."

Kai turned, then stopped at the door.

"I thought you understood. But you're just like everyone else. Too scared to act. Too comfortable to care."

Eli didn't respond.

Kai walked out. The bell jingled behind him.

He didn't look back.

By the time Kai returned to his apartment, he was shaking. Not from fear—rage.

Eli had given up. Chosen comfort. And Kai was done listening to people who wanted him to stop.

He dropped onto the futon, opened the scanner app. More patrols. More chatter. The net was tightening.

His phone buzzed.

Sienna: I'm serious about meeting. I can help. But only if you let me.

Kai stared at it.

He typed:

I can't stop. Not until Grayson's held accountable. You know that.

The reply came fast:

Then let me help you do it the right way. Legally. Before you get yourself killed.

Kai set the phone down. Stood. Walked to the door.

He could meet Sienna. Try to work with her.

Or keep going. Alone.

He opened the door and walked into the hallway.

He'd made his choice.

Dawn

Kai stood on the rooftop, watching the sunrise stain the city orange and gold. Sirens echoed in the distance. The wind carried the scent of rain.

He hadn't slept. Couldn't.

Eli was gone. Sienna was closing in. The cops were hunting him.

And he was alone.

No mentor. No allies. No lifelines.

Just him. And the mission.

He pulled out his phone. Two addresses left. Two possible Grayson sites. Two final shots at ending this.

Then, maybe, he could disappear. Or maybe not.

He pocketed the phone and turned away from the sunrise.

Symbols didn't get nights off. Even if they had to work alone.

Chapter 27
The Breakthrough

Sienna sat in the task force war room, staring at the frozen image on the monitor: Kai DuMoire's face, caught in a slice of sodium light, eyes raised toward the unseen camera. Unknowing. Vulnerable.

The breakthrough they'd been waiting for.

Around the table, the energy was sharp and electric. Captain Ortiz stood at the head, arms crossed, visibly satisfied for the first time in weeks. ADA Lee leaned forward, fingers drumming her notepad. Cole scrolled through footage on his tablet. Tommy stood by the screen, remote in hand.

"This is excellent work, Detective Halbrook," Ortiz said. "Facial ID, tools, signature message—it's airtight. We can move."

Tommy nodded. "Facial recognition confirms the ID at ninety-four percent. Kai DuMoire. Twenty-six. Brennan's Restoration Shop. No criminal record."

Lee's pen tapped twice. "How soon can we pick him up?"

"I can have a warrant by the end of the day," Ortiz replied. "Clean arrest. Low media noise."

Sienna's stomach turned. Less than twenty-four hours.

"Wait," she said.

The room paused. Eyes on her.

"We should take our time. Double-check everything. We only get one shot. If anything's off—if the defense challenges the footage—we could lose him entirely."

Ortiz raised a brow. "The footage is clear. What's your concern?"

"Entrapment claims. The decoy vehicle. The setup. A defense attorney could spin it. Say we induced the crime."

Lee shook her head. "Entrapment requires coercion. We didn't pressure him—we gave him a window. That's legal."

"Legal, yes. But risky. If it becomes a public relations disaster, the Ghost becomes a martyr. That's a bigger problem."

Ortiz crossed his arms. "What do you want?"

"More time. Forty-eight hours of surveillance. Confirm whether he's working alone. If there's a network, we need to know."

Cole looked up. "You think he has support?"

"I don't know. But if we arrest him now, we lose the chance to find out."

Lee exhaled. "The mayor's office wants movement. Public interest is high. Grayson's lawyers are trying to spin him as a scape-goat. We need results."

Sienna held her ground. "And we'll get them. But let's do it right."

Ortiz studied her. "Forty-eight hours. No more. Then we move."

Sienna nodded. "Understood."

"Tommy, send the footage package to my office. Cole, work the surveillance plan with Halbrook. Lee, start the paperwork. We go in two days."

The meeting ended. Ortiz and Lee left. Tommy gathered his gear. Cole lingered.

"You okay?" he asked quietly.

"I'm fine."

"You just bought the Ghost two more days. Why?"

"I want the full picture."

"Or you don't want to catch him?"

Sienna met his gaze. "We do this right. No shortcuts."

Cole nodded slowly. "Just be careful. If Ortiz or Lee think you're stalling, it's your badge on the line."

He left. Sienna turned back to the monitor.

Kai's face stared back. Not a criminal. Just a kid trying to fix something that was broken.

She wasn't sure if she was about to save him—or betray everything she stood for.

That afternoon, Sienna sat in her car outside Brennan's Restoration Shop. Two hours watching. Waiting.

She scrolled through the footage again. Kai approaching the decoy SUV. His hands steady. His movements careful. The message on the windshield: **DO MORE**.

It wasn't a signature.

It was a manifesto.

Her phone buzzed.

I know you're watching me. We need to talk. Old train station. Tonight. 10 p.m.

Kai.

She stared at the message. He knew.

How do I know you won't run? she texted.

Because I'm tired of running. And because I think you understand what I'm trying to do.

She did.

I'll be there.

That evening, the USB drive sat untouched on her coffee table. A copy of the surveillance footage. The case file. Everything needed for an arrest.

She hadn't sent it.

Cole called.

"You okay?"

"I'm thinking."

"About what happens next?"

"Yeah."

"Arrest him. That's what's next. That's the job."

"What if arresting him doesn't fix the problem?"

"Then fix the system. But don't break the law to do it."

He hung up.

Sienna stared at the USB drive.

Then she grabbed her jacket.

10 p.m. – Old Train Station

Abandoned. Quiet. Crumbling.

Sienna stepped inside.

Kai stood near the edge of the platform, arms loose at his sides. Tired. Worn. Determined.

"Detective Halbrook."

"Kai."

"You came."

"I came."

"You've seen the footage."

"Yes."

"Then you know it's over."

"Not yet."

He met her eyes. "We want the same thing."

"To stop Grayson?"

"To stop the suffering."

"Then why break the law?"

"Because the law hasn't worked. You've seen it. You know it."

"There are better ways."

"Are there? Because no one else is acting. I am."

"It's reckless."

"It's necessary."

"You're making yourself a target. You'll go to prison."

"I know."

They stood in silence.

"I'm building a case against Grayson," Sienna said. "Legit. Financial crimes. It'll hold up."

"How long?"

"Too long."

"I have two more locations," Kai said. "Then I'm done."

"I can't let you go."

"Then help me. Two days. That's all I need."

She stared at him. The law. The case. Her badge.

And the animals.

"Forty-eight hours," she said. "You give me everything. Documentation. Proof. No improvising. And then you disappear."

Kai exhaled. "You're serious."

"Deadly."

"If I mess up?"

"I arrest you myself."

He nodded. "Deal."

"Then go. And don't make me regret this."

Kai disappeared into the dark.

Sienna stood alone on the platform, wondering if she'd just made the worst mistake of her life—or the first right one in a long time.

Chapter 28
Unmasked

Mina Torres sat at her desk in the newsroom, staring at her email inbox. It was 9:47 a.m., and she'd already received 23 messages since she'd arrived. Most were tips about the Ghost—sightings, theories, speculation. The usual noise.

But one email stood out.

The subject line was simple: **You'll want to see this.**

No sender name. Just an anonymous Gmail account. No message in the body. Just an attachment.

Mina hesitated, her cursor hovering over the file. Anonymous tips were always risky. Could be a hoax. Could be malware.

But her instincts told her this was different.

She clicked the attachment.

The image loaded slowly. A still frame from what looked like surveillance footage. Grainy. Dark. But clear enough.

A figure in a parking lot. Hooded. Crouched next to a car. Tools in hand. And his face—partially visible in profile, illuminated by a streetlight.

The Ghost.

Mina felt her breath catch. This wasn't a blurry phone video. This was high-resolution surveillance footage. Professional. Official.

This was from the police.

She zoomed in on the face. Young. Male. Mid-twenties. Dark hair. Sharp features.

Not a myth. Not a legend. A real person.

And someone had leaked his image to her.

Mina's phone rang. Her editor, Derek.

"Torres, my office. Now."

Derek Huang sat behind his desk, arms crossed. On his computer monitor, the same image Mina had received was displayed in full screen.

"Tell me you got this too," he said when Mina walked in.

"I did. About ten minutes ago."

"Anonymous sender?"

"Yeah. Gmail account. No message. Just the attachment."

Derek leaned back. "I got the same thing. So did three other journalists I've talked to this morning. Someone's leaking this. And they want it out there."

Mina stared at the image. "This is police surveillance footage. Has to be. Look at the quality. The angle."

"Which means someone inside the department is leaking it. The question is why."

"To put pressure on the Ghost. To force him into the open. Or to force the department to act."

Derek nodded. "Either way, this is a story. A big one. 'The Ghost Has a Face.' We run it, we're front page. We're trending."

Mina felt her stomach tighten. "We don't know who he is yet. Just that he exists. Is that enough?"

"It's more than we had yesterday. We run it now, we own the story."

"But what if running it puts him in danger? What if it helps the police catch him?"

Derek gave her a sharp look. "Since when do you care about protecting sources?"

"He's not a source. He's a subject."

"He's a vigilante. Breaking the law. And our job is to report the news. Not to decide who deserves protection."

Mina didn't respond. Because Derek was right. Her job was to report. To inform. Not to protect people who broke the law.

But this felt different.

"I want you to write it," Derek said. "The Ghost Has a Face: New Evidence Reveals the Man Behind the Myth.' 800 words. I want it by noon."

"Derek—"

"This isn't a debate, Torres. This is news. And we're running it. With or without you."

Mina stared at him, then at the image on the screen. The Ghost's face. Vulnerable. Human.

She nodded. "I'll have it to you by noon."

Mina sat at her desk, staring at the blank document. The cursor blinked. Waiting.

She'd written dozens of articles about the Ghost. Had built his legend. But always, he'd been a myth. A shadow. A symbol.

Now he was a person. And Mina had to decide how to tell that story.

She started typing.

The Ghost Has a Face: New Evidence Reveals the Man Behind the Myth

By Mina Torres

For months, the Ghost Rescuer has operated in the shadows, saving animals while evading law enforcement. His methods were precise. His motives were clear. But his identity remained a mystery.

Until now.

New surveillance footage obtained by *The Chronicle* shows the Ghost's face for the first time—a young man, mid-twenties, captured during a rescue operation at Riverside Park. The image, believed to be from a police sting operation, reveals a figure who is neither superhero nor villain, but something more complicated: a person.

The Ghost's campaign has sparked fierce debate. Activists hail him as a necessary force. Law enforcement warns of the dangers of vigilantism. And the public remains divided.

But one thing is now clear: the Ghost is real. And he's running out of time.

Sources close to the investigation say police are closing in. The leaked image suggests the department has identified him, though no official statement has been released.

The question now is not whether the Ghost will be caught, but when.

Mina stopped typing, read what she'd written. It was good. Balanced. Informative. It didn't reveal his identity, but it confirmed he was real.

It was journalism.

But it also felt like a betrayal.

She saved the draft, stood, and walked to the window. The newsroom buzzed around her—phones ringing, keyboards clacking. The machinery of news, grinding forward.

Her phone buzzed. A text from an unknown number.

I saw the image. Please don't run it. Not yet. I need more time.

Mina stared at the message. The Ghost. Kai.

He was asking her not to publish. Asking her to protect him.

But that wasn't her job.

She typed a reply.

I don't have a choice. The story's already out there. Other outlets are running it. If I don't publish, someone else will.

The response came quickly.

Then you're helping them catch me. You know that, right?

Mina felt her chest tighten. *I'm doing my job.*

Your job is to tell the truth. The truth is that the system is failing. But you're not writing that story. You're writing the story they want you to write.

Mina stared at the message. He was right. She was writing the story the system wanted. The story that would help the police catch him.

But what was the alternative? Suppress the image? Refuse to publish?

She typed a reply.

I'm sorry. But this is news. And I have to report it.

The response took longer this time.

Then I hope it was worth it.

Mina set the phone down, stared at the draft. She could delete it. Could refuse to publish.

But Derek would just assign it to someone else. And the story would run anyway.

She hit send, submitted the draft, and walked away from her desk.

By 1 p.m., the article was live. By 2 p.m., it was trending on social media. By 3 p.m., it had been picked up by national outlets.

The Ghost Has a Face.

Mina sat in a coffee shop across from the newsroom, watching the reactions pour in. Twitter was exploding—#GhostRescuer was trending, with over 200,000 tweets. Reddit threads were multiplying, amateur detectives analyzing the image pixel by pixel. Facebook groups were debating whether the Ghost was a hero or a criminal.

The image was everywhere—shared, analyzed, enhanced, speculated upon. Someone had already run it through facial recognition software. Someone else had created a comparison chart with local locksmith apprentices.

The myth was collapsing. The Ghost was becoming human. Vulnerable. Exposed.

And the hunt was intensifying.

Claudia Reyes had posted a statement calling for the Ghost to be protected. The post had been shared 50,000 times.

Officer Lin had issued a counter-statement warning that vigilantism was dangerous and illegal.

ADA Lee had given a press conference calling the leak "a serious breach of protocol" and promising an arrest "in the near future."

And Mina was at the center of it all. Her article. Her byline. Her decision.

Her inbox was flooded. Some praising her journalism. Some condemning her for helping the police. Some threatening her for "betraying" the Ghost.

She'd built the Ghost's myth. And now she was watching it burn.

Her phone rang. A number she didn't recognize.

"Hello?"

"Ms. Torres, this is Detective Sienna Halbrook. We need to talk."

Mina felt her stomach drop. "About what?"

"About the image you published. About what you know."

"I'm a journalist. I don't reveal sources."

"I'm not asking you to. I'm asking you to meet me. Off the record. Because I think we both want the same thing."

"And what's that?"

"To make sure the Ghost doesn't get himself killed."

Mina was quiet. "Where?"

"Old train station. 6 p.m. Come alone."

The line went dead.

Mina set the phone down. The article was still trending. The image was still spreading. The Ghost was still being hunted.

And Mina had helped make it happen.

6 p.m. - Old Train Station

The old train station was abandoned, a relic from the city's industrial past. Mina parked her car and walked to the platform, where Detective Halbrook was waiting.

"Thanks for coming," Sienna said.

"You said this was about the Ghost."

"It is. I need to know who leaked that image to you."

"I told you. I don't reveal sources."

"I'm not asking as a cop. I'm asking as someone who's trying to protect him."

Mina stared at her. "You're trying to protect him? You're the one hunting him."

"I'm trying to catch him before someone else does. Before he does something that gets him killed. But that image you published? It's made my job harder. Because now everyone's looking for him. Not just the police. The public. Activists. And some of them don't have his best interests at heart."

Mina felt her chest tighten. "I didn't have a choice. The image was already out there. If I didn't publish, someone else would have."

"I know. But now the clock's ticking. And I need to find him before someone else does."

"Why are you telling me this?"

"Because I think you care about what happens to him. And I think you can help me."

"How?"

"By not publishing anything else. By giving me time to bring him in safely. By trusting that I'm trying to do the right thing."

Mina studied her. "You're asking me to suppress news."

"I'm asking you to be responsible. To think about the consequences of what you publish. To recognize that journalism isn't just about reporting facts. It's about understanding impact."

Mina was quiet. "What happens if I say no?"

"Then the Ghost keeps running. Keeps taking risks. And sooner or later, he gets caught. Or killed. And you'll have to live with knowing you could have prevented it."

Mina stared at her. "That's not fair."

"No. It's not. But it's the truth."

Sienna turned, walked away, leaving Mina alone on the platform.

Mina stood there, staring at the rusted tracks, the cracked concrete, the graffiti-covered walls.

She'd built the Ghost's myth. Had amplified his story. Had turned him into a symbol.

And now that symbol was being hunted. And Mina didn't know how to stop it.

She pulled out her phone, stared at the article. The image. The comments. The shares.

The Ghost Has a Face.

And Mina had given it to the world.

She just hoped it wouldn't get him killed.

Chapter 29
Burning Bridges

Kai sat on the rooftop of his building, staring at his phone, at the image that was everywhere now. His face. Partially visible. Captured in profile. Exposed.

The Ghost Has a Face.

The headline was on every news site. Every social media platform. Every screen in the city.

He'd been careful. So careful. Months of operating in the shadows, leaving no trace, staying invisible. And now, in a single moment, all of that was gone.

Someone had leaked the surveillance footage. Someone inside the police department.

And Mina had published it.

Kai set the phone down, staring out over the horizon. The city stretched below him—a grid of lights and shadows. But now it felt different. Smaller. Like the walls were closing in.

He'd read Mina's article. Had seen her justification. *This is news. And I have to report it.*

But it wasn't just news. It was a target. A beacon. A signal to everyone in the city: here he is. Come and get him.

Kai pulled his hood up, even though no one could see him up here. The gesture felt futile. Because the hood didn't matter anymore. The shadows didn't matter. The myth was collapsing. And Kai was becoming real.

And real meant vulnerable.

His phone buzzed. A text from Sienna:

I know you're scared. But I can help. Meet me. Let's figure this out together.

Kai stared at the message. Sienna wanted to help. But helping meant stopping. Surrendering.

And he couldn't do that. Not while Grayson was still out there.

He pocketed the phone, stood, and walked to the edge of the rooftop. The wind was cool, sharp with the smell of rain and exhaust. Below, the city hummed with life—cars on the highway, lights flickering in apartment windows, the distant wail of sirens.

He used to feel powerful up here. Like he could see everything. Like he could make a difference.

Now he just felt small.

Kai moved through the streets, hood up, head down. Every person he passed felt like a threat. Every glance felt like recognition. Every siren felt like it was coming for him.

The image was everywhere. On phones. On screens. On posters taped to light poles by activists who wanted to protect him—and critics who wanted him caught.

The Ghost Has a Face.

Kai turned into an alley, disappearing into shadow. He had two options: run, or finish what he started. Shut down Grayson's operations. Free the animals.

Even if it meant getting caught.

He pulled out his phone, opened the map. Two locations left. Two final targets.

The net was closing. Time was running out.

. . .

Brennan's Restoration Shop was dark. Closed. The sign flipped. The door locked.

Kai peered through the glass. Empty benches. Bare racks. Eli was gone.

He picked the lock, stepped inside.

Silence.

The shop felt hollow. Like a body without a soul.

A note on the counter in Eli's handwriting:

Kai,

I'm sorry. But I can't be part of this anymore. The police came by. Showed me the image. They know you're connected to me. And I can't risk my business. My freedom.

You can't fight the whole city. You can't win this battle alone. And I can't watch you destroy yourself trying.

— Eli

Kai read the note twice. Then again. The words landed like lead.

Eli had walked away.

He crumpled the paper and left.

Back at his apartment, Kai packed. Tools. Clothes. Cash. Everything he might need to disappear.

Because maybe Eli was right. Maybe the city was too big. Too armored. Too corrupt.

Maybe it was time to stop.

But Grayson was still out there. Still hurting animals. Still protected by lawyers and silence.

And Kai was the only one who could stop him.

He sat down, pulled up the map. Two red pins. Two operations.

He could run. Or he could finish this.

Kai zipped the bag, set it aside, and walked to the window.

He wasn't running.

. . .

That night, Kai returned to the rooftop. The wind sliced colder now. The city lights looked harder. Meaner.

He scrolled through his messages. Sienna again:

I can help. Don't do this alone.

He typed:

I'm going to finish this. With or without you.

She replied instantly:

Don't. You'll get caught. Let me help you do this legally.

Kai hesitated, then wrote:

The system doesn't work. You know that.

A pause. Then:

Then let me be there. To keep you safe.

He stared at the screen, then wrote:

I work alone.

He pocketed the phone.

This wasn't about survival. This was about truth. About justice. About saving what could be saved.

He remembered his father—idealistic, relentless, destroyed by the same system Kai was now fighting. Eli had warned him: *You're making the same mistakes.*

But Kai couldn't stop. Not when sixty animals had already been saved. Not when others still needed him.

Even if it meant losing everything.

Midnight

Kai burned his notes. Maps. Names. Evidence. One page at a time, feeding it into the fire.

Erasing the Ghost.

He cleared his phone. Deleted everything. Wiped the drive. Left nothing behind.

Just in case.

Then he slung the duffel bag over his shoulder and turned off the lights.

He didn't look back.

Dawn

Kai stood one last time on the rooftop, watching the city stretch beneath him.

He had memorized the two addresses. The final rescues.

No more doubt. No more hiding.

No more chances.

He pulled up his hood and headed for the stairs.

He would finish what he started.

Even if no one remembered.

Even if no one cared.

Because he couldn't do nothing.

Not now.

Chapter 30
Crossroads

Sienna sat in her apartment, staring at the television. The news was running the story on loop. The leaked image. Kai's face. The speculation. The manhunt.

The Ghost Has a Face.

Every channel was covering it. The city was obsessed.

And Sienna was at the center of it.

She'd set the trap. Captured the footage. Identified Kai. And now the whole city was hunting him.

Her phone buzzed. A text from Cole:

We're closing in. Ortiz wants to move tomorrow morning. Don't blow this.

Sienna stared at the message. Tomorrow morning. Less than twelve hours.

She typed a reply:

Understood.

But she didn't understand. Not really. Because everything about this felt wrong.

Kai wasn't a criminal. He was someone trying to do the right thing in a system that was failing. And Sienna was about to arrest him for it.

She turned off the television, walked to the window. The city stretched out below her—lights, motion, shadows.

Somewhere out there, Kai was hiding. Planning.

And Sienna had to decide: was she going to catch him—or protect him?

The apartment felt too small. Sienna paced.

She'd become a cop to help people. To protect the vulnerable. But what happened when the law protected the guilty and punished the just?

She thought about Grayson. The puppy mills. The lawyers. The endless complaints that led nowhere.

She'd given ADA Lee everything. And Lee had said it would take months. Maybe years. Meanwhile, animals continued to suffer.

The system protected people like Grayson. And it punished people like Kai.

Kai had stepped in where the law had failed. Sixty animals freed. Illegal? Yes. Necessary? Absolutely.

Her phone buzzed again.

Cole: *You okay? You've been quiet.*

Sienna replied:

I'm fine. Just thinking.

Cole: *About the Ghost?*

About everything.

Cole: *Don't overthink this. We have a job to do. We do it. That's all.*

She set the phone down. Cole made it sound so simple.

But it wasn't.

· · ·

Her phone rang. Ortiz.

"Detective Halbrook."

"Sienna. We need to talk. About tomorrow. The arrest. Making sure it goes smoothly."

"I'm ready."

"Are you? Cole says you've been stalling. Dragging your feet. I need to know—are you with us, or with him?"

"I'm with the law."

"The law says he's a criminal. That we arrest him. Are you willing to do that?"

Sienna paused. "Yes."

"Good. Because tomorrow morning, we move. I want you leading the arrest. Understood?"

"Understood."

He hung up.

Sienna sat in silence. Tomorrow. The arrest. The end of the Ghost.

But not of Grayson.

Kai would be crucified. Grayson would walk free.

The system would win. The animals would lose.

Sienna walked to the window.

She pulled out her phone and read Kai's last message:

I'm going to finish this. With or without you. I have two locations left. I'm shutting them down. Tonight.

If she waited until morning, it would all be over—wrong.

Unless she found him first.

She grabbed her jacket, badge, and keys. Paused at the door.

This was the crossroads.

Stay and follow orders. Or act. Step outside. Help him finish what he started.

Sienna was tired of watching the system fail.

She locked the door and left.

. . .

She drove through the city, checking the map. Two properties left—Grayson's suspected sites. One on the east side. One near the docks.

She headed east.

The warehouse was dark. No lights. No movement.

Sienna parked a block away, approached on foot. Industrial. Isolated.

She texted Kai:

I know where you are. Don't do this alone. Let me help.

No response.

She crept toward the building, peered through a window.

Cages. Dozens. Dogs, cats, rabbits. Cramped. Filthy.

Kai was already inside.

She saw him moving—quiet, efficient, unlocking cages.

Too efficient.

She called him. He answered on the third ring. "What?"

"Get out. Now. It's a trap."

"What are you—"

Floodlights snapped on. Sirens. Shouts.

"Police! Freeze!"

Sienna's heart dropped.

She ran to the perimeter, flashing her badge.

"Detective Halbrook. What's going on?"

An officer turned. "Anonymous tip. The Ghost is here. Building's surrounded."

A setup.

Inside, Kai stood among open cages. He'd freed them all.

But now—sirens. Lights. Orders shouted over megaphones.

He ran to the exit. Opened the door—and froze.

Floodlights. Officers. Rifles.

"Hands up!"

Kai raised his hands slowly.

Then he saw her—Sienna. Just beyond the cordon. Relief and regret on her face.

She'd tried to warn him.

Too late.

Sienna pushed forward, badge raised. "Stand down. He's mine."

"Detective—"

"My case. My arrest. I'm taking him in."

They hesitated. Then backed off.

She approached Kai. Pulled out cuffs. Met his eyes.

"Trust me," she whispered.

She cuffed him. Walked him to her car. Drove away.

Silence.

Kai sat in the back seat, handcuffed.

"Where are you taking me?"

"Somewhere safe."

"I'm under arrest."

"No. You're not."

Kai met her eyes in the mirror. "What are you doing?"

"Saving you. From yourself. From the system. From Grayson."

"Why?"

"Because you're right. The system's broken. And I'm tired of pretending it's not."

She pulled into an abandoned garage. Stopped. Turned around.

"I'm going to uncuff you. Then we shut down Grayson's last operation. Together. Legally. By the book."

"You're serious."

"Dead serious. But if you screw up, I *will* arrest you."

"Understood."

She uncuffed him. Handed him his tools.

Kai nodded. "Thank you."

"Don't thank me yet. We're not done."

She started the car.

The Ghost and the Detective. On the same side now.

An uneasy alliance.

But maybe, just maybe, the start of something better.

Chapter 31
Convergence

Sienna sat in her car in the abandoned parking garage, engine off, watching Kai in the rearview mirror. He rubbed his wrists where the cuffs had been, his face a mix of confusion and cautious hope.

"You're serious about this," he said. Not a question.

"I'm serious."

"You're risking everything. Your career. Your reputation. Maybe your freedom."

"I know."

"Why?"

Sienna turned in her seat. "Because you're right. The system is failing. And I'm tired of being part of the problem."

Kai studied her. "What's the plan?"

"We finish what you started. Shut down Grayson's last operation. Document everything. Build an airtight case. And hand it over to someone outside this corrupt system—federal prosecutors, the Attorney General. Someone Grayson can't buy."

Kai nodded. "And what happens to me?"

"If we succeed, maybe the department backs off. Maybe you walk."

"And if we fail?"

"Then we both go to prison."

He was quiet. "Bad odds."

"The only ones we've got."

Kai met her eyes. "All right. Let's do it."

Sienna started the car and pulled out of the garage.

They drove in silence. Past midnight. The streets were mostly empty, the air damp.

"Where's the last site?" Sienna asked.

"Storage facility near the docks. Grayson owns it through a shell company. I tracked shipments—saw cages moved in last week. Big ones."

"You sure it's still active?"

"I can feel it. The animals. Their distress. It's like a signal."

She glanced at him. "Your empathy. How does it work?"

Kai hesitated. "It's hard to explain. I feel what they feel. Pain. Fear. Helplessness. Not in words—just... sensations."

"That sounds exhausting."

"It is. But it's also why I can't stop. Once you know they're suffering, you can't look away."

Sienna understood. Not through empathy—but exposure. Through every form the system had failed to act on.

"Security?"

"Cameras. Motion sensors. Maybe guards. Grayson's not taking chances anymore."

"Then we're smart. We move fast. Document everything."

Kai nodded. "Agreed."

. . .

They parked a block away, sheltered by an old warehouse. Before getting out, Sienna turned to him.

"If we do this... it has to be the last time. After tonight, you stop. Walk away."

Kai didn't answer right away. "Every time I try to walk away, I feel them. The suffering. I don't know if I can."

"You have to. Or you'll end up like your father. Alone. Burned out. Destroyed."

His jaw tensed. "You know about him?"

"I'm a detective. He fought for what he believed in. Died bitter. Isolated. Because he couldn't let go."

"He died doing what mattered."

"And it consumed him."

Kai stared out the window. "So what do I do instead?"

"Work with the law. Build cases. Change it from the inside. It's slower. But it lasts."

He was quiet for a long beat. "Okay. After tonight, I'm done. I walk away."

"Promise?"

"Promise."

Sienna nodded. "Let's finish this."

They approached the facility on foot. Three stories. Loading docks. Security cameras. Lights glowing inside.

Sienna opened her camera app. "We record everything. Every violation. Every cage. This is evidence."

Kai pulled out his lockpicks. "Side door, near the loading dock. No cameras."

The lock clicked. They slipped in.

The smell hit them instantly—urine, feces, rot. Rows of cages lined the walls, animals crammed inside. Dogs barked hoarsely. Cats hissed. Rabbits sat silent, eyes glazed.

It was worse than the first raid.

Kai staggered, hit by a wave of empathic distress.

"You okay?" Sienna asked.

"Yeah. Just... it's a lot."

"Can you do this?"

"I have to."

Sienna documented everything. The cages. The serial numbers. Breeding logs. Shipment invoices tied to Grayson's shell company.

Kai freed the animals, fast but careful. Dogs scattered. Cats bolted into the shadows.

But something was off.

Too quiet. No guards. No workers.

A trap.

Sienna felt it too. Her instincts screamed. "We need to move."

Then came the sirens. Floodlights. Voices.

"Police! Hands in the air!"

Kai spun to her. "What do we do?"

"Run. Now."

They dashed for the exit—but were met by a wall of officers.

Guns drawn.

"Freeze!"

Sienna raised her badge. "Detective Halbrook! Stand down!"

The officers hesitated. Then Captain Ortiz stepped through.

"What the hell is this, Detective?"

Sienna faced him. "We have evidence—Grayson's operation. Illegal. We needed to act."

Ortiz's voice was ice. "You were supposed to lead an arrest tomorrow. Instead, you're breaking and entering with a suspect. You've gone rogue."

"The system failed. We didn't."

He turned to the officers. "Arrest them both."

· · ·

Sienna and Kai sat in separate squad cars. Handcuffed. Silent.

From her window, she saw Cole. He looked stricken. Angry.

He opened her door. "What were you thinking?"

"That animals were dying. And no one was doing anything."

"You threw away your career."

"Maybe. But I did something."

He stared at her. "You really believe this was worth it?"

"Yes."

He closed the door and walked away.

An hour later, Sienna sat cuffed in the precinct's interrogation room.

Ortiz and ADA Lee stood across from her.

"You're facing serious charges," Lee said. "Breaking and entering. Obstruction. Aiding a fugitive."

"I was building a case. I was doing my job."

"Your job is to follow the law."

"And what if the law is broken? What if it protects people like Grayson while punishing those trying to stop him?"

Ortiz exhaled. "You crossed a line, Sienna. You're suspended. And the DA may press charges."

"What about Kai?"

"He's being processed. Multiple charges."

"He saved lives. He exposed Grayson. He did what we couldn't."

"And now it may all be inadmissible," Lee snapped. "Because it was obtained illegally. You made it harder to prosecute Grayson. Not easier."

Sienna stared at them both. "So you're saying it was all for nothing."

Lee gathered her things. "I'm saying you should pray the DA goes easy. Turn in your badge and your weapon."

She left.

Ortiz lingered, his voice heavy. "I'm sorry. But you left me no choice."

DuMoire

He walked out.
Sienna sat alone.
Suspended. Disgraced. Possibly facing charges.
But she didn't regret it.
Because she'd acted.
And sometimes, that had to be enough.

Chapter 32
The Meeting
Kai

Kai sat in the holding cell, staring at the concrete walls, the fluorescent lights buzzing overhead. Three hours in. Processed. Fingerprinted. Photographed. Charged with multiple counts of breaking and entering, trespassing, vandalism.

The Ghost was caught.

He thought about the animals—the ones he'd saved. Sixty rescues in three months. Sixty lives that would have been lost without him.

But now he was in a cell. And Grayson was still free. Still operating. Still protected.

Had it been worth it?

Kai didn't know anymore.

The door opened. A guard stepped in. "You've got a visitor."

Kai looked up. "Who?"

"Detective Halbrook. She's in the interview room. Says she needs to talk to you."

Kai stood slowly. Sienna. The detective who'd arrested him. Helped him. Risked everything for him. And now she wanted to talk.

Why?

. . .

Sienna

Sienna sat in the interview room, waiting. Suspended. Stripped of her badge and gun. Facing criminal charges. Her career—over.

But before everything moved too far, she needed to see Kai. One last conversation. One last truth.

The door opened. Kai stepped in, wrists cuffed, tired in every way a person could be tired.

The guard uncuffed him, stepped out, and closed the door.

They stared at each other across the table.

"Why are you here?" Kai asked.

"Because I need to understand," Sienna said. "Why you did it. Why you kept going, even knowing you'd get caught."

Kai was quiet. "Because I had to. Because the animals were suffering. Because the system wasn't working. And I couldn't look away."

"And now? Was it worth it?"

Kai looked away. "I don't know. I saved sixty animals. But Grayson's still out there. And now I'm here. And you... you might lose everything. So maybe it wasn't worth it. Maybe I just made things worse."

"You didn't make things worse," she said. "You forced the city to pay attention. Before you, Grayson was untouchable. Now? Everyone knows what he's done."

"But did I *change* anything? Or just... collapse a myth?"

"You saved sixty animals. That's not nothing."

Kai met her eyes. "But what about the ones I didn't save?"

"You can't save them all. No one can. And trying will destroy you. Just like it destroyed your father."

He flinched. "He died fighting for what he believed in."

"He died alone. Bitter. Burned out. Because he couldn't let go. Because he believed he had to do it all himself."

Kai's voice was low. "So what, I'm supposed to give up?"

"No. You're supposed to fight smarter. Use the law. Build cases. Work *with* people, not around them."

He gave a dry smile. "Like you?"

"Yeah. Like me."

Kai studied her. "You've lost everything for this."

"I haven't lost what matters," she said. "My integrity. My purpose. That's why I joined in the first place. Somewhere along the way, I started enforcing laws instead of seeking justice. You reminded me of the difference."

Kai

Kai leaned back. "What now?"

"We finish it. The evidence we gathered—videos, logs, records—I uploaded it all to a secure server before they arrested us. And I sent it out. To federal prosecutors. Journalists. Animal welfare groups. Everyone who might actually do something."

"But Lee said it wouldn't hold up."

"Lee might be compromised. The local system won't touch Grayson. That's why we went federal."

"You really think they'll act?"

"I think it's our best shot."

Kai stared at her. "And what about us?"

Sienna didn't flinch. "If we're lucky, the federal case overshadows the charges. They drop it all. If not—we face the consequences."

Kai exhaled slowly. "Some plan."

"It's all we've got."

He was quiet for a long beat. "Why are you doing this? Why risk your career—your life—for me?"

"I'm not doing it *for* you," Sienna said. "I'm doing it because it's the right thing. Because animals are suffering. Because someone has to act. You started it. I'm helping finish it."

Kai gave a faint smile. "You sound like me."

"Maybe. But I'm doing it by the book."

"We both ended up in handcuffs."

Sienna tilted her head. "Maybe the system doesn't know what to do with people who do the right thing the wrong way."

The door opened. The guard stepped in. "Time's up."

Kai stood, held out his wrists.

The guard re-cuffed him.

"Kai," Sienna said softly.

He turned back.

"Thank you. For doing what I couldn't. For making people see."

He nodded. "Thank *you*. For trying to fix it."

The guard led him out.

Sienna sat alone, staring at her phone.

She'd crossed a line. Broken the rules. Lost her badge.

But maybe she'd found something else.

Sienna

Outside, she sat in her car under the sodium-orange lights of the precinct parking lot. Her phone buzzed.

An email.

From: Assistant U.S. Attorney James Chen

Subject: Re: Leonard Grayson

Detective Halbrook,

Thank you for bringing this to our attention. We are opening a federal investigation into Leonard Grayson and the affiliated properties.

This matter may involve violations of the Animal Welfare Act, tax law, and potentially RICO statutes. We'll be in contact within 24 hours.

She stared at it. Then smiled. It was working.

Her phone buzzed again. Another email. Then another. Journalists. Prosecutors. Activists.

The story was breaking.

Kai

Back in the cell, Kai lay on the bench, eyes open, staring at the ceiling.

He thought about Sienna. About her risk. Her choice.

He wasn't alone anymore.

Maybe, just maybe, they had done enough.

Maybe the system would listen this time.

Maybe.

But for now, all they could do was wait.

Chapter 33
Three Weeks Later
Mina

Mina Torres stood outside the federal courthouse, watching Leonard Grayson being led up the steps in handcuffs. Camera flashes exploded. Reporters shouted questions. Protesters held signs: **JUSTICE FOR ANIMALS** and **GRAYSON: COUNCIL MEMBER OR CRIMINAL?**

Three weeks. That's how long it had taken for everything to change.

Her article had gone viral within hours. By morning, every major news outlet was covering the story. By noon, federal agents were executing search warrants. By evening, Grayson had resigned from city council.

And now, three weeks later, he was being arraigned on federal charges.

Mina lifted her phone and hit record. This was the moment. The culmination of months of reporting. The vindication of everything Kai and Sienna had risked.

Grayson's attorney—Marcus Whitfield, the same smug mouthpiece who'd once threatened half the city—walked beside him, grim now. No more confidence. Just the weight of a client facing serious federal charges.

Animal Welfare Act violations. Tax evasion. Money laundering. Racketeering.

The evidence had been overwhelming. Sienna's video footage showed such egregious conditions that even Grayson's political allies distanced themselves. The financial records tracked millions through shell companies. The breeding logs revealed years of systematic cruelty.

The federal prosecutors had moved fast. Faster than Mina expected.

Grayson disappeared into the courthouse. Mina lowered her phone.

"Hell of a story," a voice behind her said.

She turned. Derek Huang, her editor, stood there watching the crowd.

"Yeah," she said. "It is."

"You should be proud. This is the kind of journalism that matters —holding power accountable."

Mina nodded. But she didn't feel proud. She felt tired. And conflicted.

Because the story wasn't just about Grayson. It was about Kai— the Ghost. The vigilante she'd helped shape. The man who saved sixty animals while she built his myth.

"What about the Ghost?" she asked. "And Detective Halbrook?"

Derek shrugged. "That's the next story. DA's reviewing their cases. Could go either way."

She pulled out her phone. No messages from Kai. Nothing from Sienna.

She'd tried reaching out. Texts. Calls. But after their arrests, both went dark.

And she didn't blame them. She'd published the image that exposed Kai. Helped the police close in. Even if it helped lead to Grayson's arrest, it was still a betrayal.

She pocketed the phone and headed back to the newsroom.

The story wasn't over yet.

Kai

Kai sat in the jail's visitation room. Three weeks in. No more holding cell—he'd been moved to general population while awaiting trial.

Three weeks of fluorescent lights, concrete walls, and the hum of constant voices. Three weeks of silence. Of waiting. Of wondering if Sienna's gamble had worked.

Today, something changed.

His public defender, Sarah Chen—a tired woman with dark eyes and no time for pleasantries—had called for an emergency meeting. Said she had news.

Good news.

The door opened. Sarah walked in with a folder, her face unreadable.

"Good news?" Kai asked.

Sarah sat across from him and opened the folder. "The DA's office is dropping all charges."

Kai blinked. "What?"

"All of it. Breaking and entering, trespassing, vandalism. You're being released."

"How? Why?"

She slid the document across the table. "Federal prosecutors filed a motion saying you and Detective Halbrook acted as whistleblowers. That you were documenting ongoing criminal activity the local authorities ignored. The DA reviewed the evidence and dropped the case."

Kai skimmed the paper. Dense legal text, but the last line said everything: **All charges dismissed.**

"So... I'm free?"

"You are. Processing should be done within the hour."

He exhaled. "And Sienna?"

"Same. Her charges are being dropped too. Whistleblower protection."

Relief hit like a wave. The pressure that had sat in his chest for weeks suddenly lifted.

"And Grayson?" he asked.

Sarah smiled. "Arraigned this morning. Federal charges—Animal Welfare Act, tax evasion, money laundering, RICO. He's looking at twenty years. Maybe more."

Kai leaned back. Twenty years. For a man who'd operated with impunity for years.

"So... we won."

"You won," she said. "You and Detective Halbrook. You saved those animals. You forced the system to act."

"And the animals from the storage facility?"

"All in protective custody. Most have been placed with rescue groups. Some already adopted. They're safe."

Kai closed his eyes. Safe. That word had never meant more.

"Thank you," he said.

Sarah gathered her files. "Thank Detective Halbrook. She made this happen. The evidence, the outreach—without that, you'd still be facing trial."

At the door, she paused. "For what it's worth, Mr. DuMoire— what you did was illegal. But it was brave. The system failed. You didn't."

She left him alone with the dismissal papers—and a future.

Three weeks ago, he was the Ghost. Hunted. Anonymous.

Now he was Kai DuMoire. Free.

Vindicated.

Sienna

Sienna stood outside the courthouse, watching the aftermath of

Grayson's arraignment. Protesters still lined the sidewalks. Cameras flashed.

It was over.

Three weeks of suspension. Three weeks of waiting. And finally —vindication.

Her phone buzzed. Ortiz.

"Detective Halbrook."

"Sienna. Just heard from the DA. Charges dropped. You're clear."

She closed her eyes. "Thank you."

"Don't thank me. Thank the feds. They called you a whistleblower."

"And my suspension?"

A pause. "You're reinstated. But on probation. Six months. You're reassigned. Community outreach. No more major crimes."

Sienna nodded slowly. A demotion in everything but name. A compromise.

"I understand."

"Report Monday. And Sienna?"

"Yeah?"

"What you did was reckless. But it was the right call. Grayson needed to be stopped. Thank you."

He hung up.

She tucked the phone away and stared at the courthouse.

Vindicated. But punished.

Still—it was better than prison. Better than losing her badge entirely.

Her phone buzzed again. A new number.

Heard the charges were dropped. Congratulations. Want to grab coffee?

She smiled.

Kai.

Coffee sounds good. When?

The reply came instantly.

Now. If you're free.
Send me the address.

The Coffee Shop

Kai sat near the window, watching the street. Just two hours out. Two hours of freedom. The air felt different.

The door opened. Sienna walked in, found him, slid into the booth.

"You look like hell," she said.

He grinned. "So do you."

They ordered black coffee. No small talk. Just silence and the weight of everything they'd been through.

"So," she asked. "What now?"

"I don't know," Kai said. "I've spent months being the Ghost. Before that, I was drifting. Not living. Just existing."

"And now?"

"Now I need to figure out who I am when I'm not hiding."

Sienna nodded. "Same."

They sipped their coffee.

"I still want to help," Kai said. "But legally. Through the system."

"I've been thinking the same. An advocacy group. Work with rescues. Build real cases. Make change the right way."

"No more breaking and entering."

"No more vigilante missions."

He smiled. "I'm in. If you'll have me."

"I'll have you," she said. "But one rule: no more solo acts. We do this together. With a team. With oversight."

"Deal," he said, and they shook.

Mina

Mina stared at her screen. The cursor blinked.

She'd tried for days to write this piece—the follow-up. But her guilt lingered. She'd helped expose Kai. Helped the police find him.

Still, this was her story to finish.

She began to type.

The Ghost and the Detective: How Two Unlikely Allies Took Down a Corrupt Council Member

By Mina Torres

For months, the city was captivated by the Ghost—a vigilante saving animals in distress. His actions were illegal. His methods controversial. But his impact? Unquestionable.

Sixty animals saved. A corrupt councilman exposed. And the public finally paying attention.

But he wasn't alone. Not in the end.

Detective Sienna Halbrook—a veteran officer—saw what others didn't: that the Ghost wasn't the problem. The system was.

Together, Kai DuMoire and Detective Halbrook risked everything. Their freedom. Their reputations. Their careers. And they won.

Grayson is facing federal charges. The animals are safe. The system was forced to act.

This isn't just a story about justice. It's about cost. About courage. About the line between law and morality—and what happens when we're brave enough to cross it.

Mina hit publish.

The comments came fast. Praise. Condemnation. Debate.

But people were talking.

That was the point.

Kai

On the rooftop one last time.

The city stretched before him. The sky deepened gold and orange. But there was no signal. No empathic pulse. Just quiet.

For the first time in months, the Ghost was silent.

He didn't need the mask anymore. Didn't need the shadows.

He had purpose. People. A path forward.

He turned, walked away from the edge, and disappeared into the city below.

Not as the Ghost.

As himself.

Sienna

Sienna sat in her car outside the precinct. Monday, she'd return to duty.

Community outreach.

Not what she'd wanted. But maybe what she needed.

Her phone buzzed.

Cole.

Welcome back. Even if it's to the kiddie table. Drinks Friday?

She smiled.

Yeah. Friday.

She drove through the city, lights blurring past.

She'd done the right thing. Even if it had cost her.

And somewhere out there, Kai was doing the same.

The Ghost was gone.

But the work was just beginning.

Chapter 34
The Aftermath
Sienna

F ive days after the emails went out, Sienna sat in a conference room at City Hall, facing the internal review board. Captain Ortiz sat to her left. ADA Lee sat across from her, flanked by two attorneys from the city's legal department.

The charges were serious: operating outside her authority, coordinating with a known vigilante, leaking evidence, compromising an active investigation.

But the evidence against Grayson was ironclad—videos, logs, invoices, animals now in protective custody. And the public support? Loud, widespread, impossible to ignore.

The city was watching. And it wanted justice.

Lee spoke first. "Detective Halbrook, your actions were reckless, unauthorized, and potentially illegal. You worked with Kai DuMoire, a vigilante who evaded arrest for months. You leaked evidence to federal authorities and the media. You ignored the chain of command."

Sienna met her eyes. "I exposed a criminal who'd operated with impunity for years. I gathered evidence now being used in federal court. I did it because the system failed—for two years. The complaints had been filed, stamped, routed—and buried."

"You broke the rules."

"The rules protected Grayson. Not the animals. Not justice."

Lee's jaw tightened. "Rules exist for a reason. Due process. Chain of custody. Protection of ongoing investigations."

"And when the rules fail? When the system shields abusers instead of victims? What then?"

"Then you work to change it from the inside. Not by taking the law into your own hands."

"I tried. I followed procedure. Filed reports. Collected evidence. And Grayson kept operating—because he had lawyers and political allies."

Silence fell.

One of the city attorneys leaned forward. "Detective Halbrook, do you regret your actions?"

Sienna paused. "I regret that the system failed. I regret that it took a vigilante and a suspended cop to stop Grayson. I regret the suffering we allowed under the banner of procedure. But do I regret stopping him? No. I don't."

Ortiz finally spoke. "Her methods were unorthodox. But her results speak for themselves. Grayson is in custody. The evidence is solid. The public backs her."

Lee's voice sharpened. "The department needs officers who follow the law. Not those who break it."

Sienna's voice was quiet. "The law failed. Someone had to act."

They deliberated. Sienna waited outside, listening to muffled voices through the door. Twenty minutes. Then thirty.

Finally, the door opened.

"Detective Halbrook," said the lead attorney, "this board has reviewed your actions. We've weighed the evidence, the circumstances, and the outcome."

Sienna braced herself.

"Your actions were unauthorized and outside departmental

protocol. You coordinated with a civilian. You leaked evidence. Under normal circumstances, this would lead to immediate termination."

Her stomach sank.

"But the circumstances were not normal. Leonard Grayson had evaded justice through political protection and legal maneuvering. Your actions resulted in a successful federal case. Animals were rescued. Public trust in law enforcement has, paradoxically, improved."

A pause.

"Therefore, the board has voted to reinstate you to active duty— with conditions."

Sienna exhaled.

"You'll be on probation for six months. You'll complete additional procedural training. Weekly oversight reports will go to Captain Ortiz. And you'll be partnered with Detective Cole Reyes to ensure compliance."

The lead attorney's gaze hardened.

"This is a second chance. There will not be a third. Do you understand?"

"I do."

"Do you accept these conditions?"

"I do."

"Then you're reinstated. Effective immediately. Report Monday morning."

"Thank you."

The board stood. Lee lingered at the table.

She said quietly, "You got lucky. The public was on your side. The feds backed you. But luck runs out. Next time, I won't be as lenient."

"There won't be a next time."

"I hope not. For your sake."

Lee left.

Ortiz and Sienna walked together to the parking garage.

"You got lucky," Ortiz said.

"I know."

"The public support saved you. Without it, you'd be charged right now."

"I know."

"Don't do it again."

"I won't have to. Grayson's done. The system finally worked."

Ortiz stopped walking. Turned.

"No. The system worked because you forced it to. Because you took a risk that could have ended your career."

Sienna raised an eyebrow. "So what are you saying?"

"I'm saying... sometimes the system needs people like you. People who care more about justice than policy. People willing to push when the boundaries protect the wrong side."

Sienna waited.

"But those people need to be smart. Strategic. They need allies. They can't go rogue."

"I understand."

Ortiz nodded. "Good. Welcome back, Detective. Don't make me regret fighting for you."

"I won't."

He walked away.

For the first time in weeks, Sienna felt something like hope.

Mina

Mina sat in her apartment, laptop open, the final article of the Ghost Rescuer series glowing on the screen.

"The Ghost, the Detective, and the System That Failed Them Both"

By Mina Torres

Three months ago, I wrote about a mysterious figure who broke into

*cars to rescue animals. I called him the Ghost Rescuer. I built a myth.
And the myth spread.*

But the truth is messier.

*Kai DuMoire isn't a hero or a villain. He's a man with an
extraordinary gift—animal empathy—who used it to save lives the
system ignored. He broke the law. But he also saved sixty animals.*

*Detective Sienna Halbrook isn't a rogue. She's a cop who
believed in the system—until it failed her. She followed protocol.
Collected evidence. Reported up the chain. And was ignored.*

*Leonard Grayson operated illegal breeding facilities for years. He
had power. Lawyers. Protection. The system shielded him.*

*So Halbrook stepped outside it. With Kai. And together, they
exposed him.*

*Was it legal? Maybe not. Was it right? That's a question we all
have to ask.*

*Grayson is now facing federal charges. The animals are safe. The
system was forced to act.*

*But it took a vigilante and a suspended detective to make it
happen.*

What does that say about the system?

*There are no easy answers. But maybe instead of hunting vigi-
lantes, we should fix the failures that create them.*

The Ghost is gone. But the questions remain.

*What do we do when the system fails? Who do we become when
the law isn't enough?*

And how do we build a world where ghosts aren't necessary?

Mina read the piece one last time, then hit publish.

Within minutes, it was trending. Praise. Backlash. Debate.

And that was the point.

Her phone buzzed. A message from an unknown number.

Thank you. For telling the truth. – K

She smiled.

Thank you. For making me think about what journalism should be. Stay safe.

I will. You too.

She closed the laptop.

She had built a myth. And now, she'd dismantled it. Told the truth—the uncomfortable, complex, necessary truth.

Maybe it was the most important thing she'd ever written.

Sienna

Monday morning.

Sienna walked into the precinct, badge on her belt, weapon at her side.

Officers nodded. Some smiled. Some looked away.

Cole stood at her desk with two coffees.

"Welcome back, partner."

"Thanks." She took a sip and sat.

"How was the hearing?"

"Reinstated. Probation. Oversight. Training. You're my babysitter."

"Could've been worse."

"Could've been better."

He grinned. "You exposed a corrupt politician. Saved animals. Kept your badge. I'd call that a win."

"I broke the rules. I risked everything."

"And you'd do it again."

She didn't answer. She didn't have to.

"What now?" he asked.

"We get back to work. There are still animals suffering. Still systems failing."

"And if the system fails again?"

Sienna looked at him. "Then we fix it. From the inside. With patience. With people."

Tommy approached, holding a tablet.

"Welcome back. You should see this."

It was Mina's article.

Sienna read it. Her chest tightened.

"She got it right," Tommy said. "Rules had become a shield for the wrong people. We have to do better."

"Yeah," Sienna said. "We do."

Her phone buzzed. A text.

Heard you're back on duty. Congrats. If you need help on any animal cases, I'm available. Legal consultation only. – Kai

She smiled and showed Cole.

"You're really bringing him in? Officially?"

"He's offering to help. Legally. The department doesn't have a say."

Cole shook his head, grinning. "You're unbelievable."

"I've been told."

She replied to Kai.

East side hoarding case. Could use your eyes. Meet me in an hour?

I'll be there.

She grabbed her jacket. "Come on. Let's go help some animals."

Cole followed. "This is going to be interesting."

"That's one word for it."

Kai

Kai arrived at the east side apartment building. Sienna and Cole were already waiting. She handed him coffee.

"Thanks for coming."

"Always. What's the situation?"

"Twelve dogs. Two cats. One-bedroom apartment. Owner says they're rescues. Neighbors say otherwise."

Kai closed his eyes. Reached out.

Distress. Fear. Sickness. All of it close. Cramped.

"They're in bad shape," he said. "Some sick. Most underfed. Owner's overwhelmed."

Sienna nodded. "Animal control's en route. We wait. Do it by the book."

They waited.

Every part of Kai wanted to act. To kick the door in. To free them.

But not anymore.

Now, the work was legal. Collaborative. Sustainable.

Animal control pulled in. Tommy stepped out.

"Ready?"

"Ready."

Inside, the woman who answered looked defensive, exhausted.

"I'm saving them. Without me, they'd be dead."

"We believe you had good intentions," Sienna said gently. "But they need more care than you can give."

The woman hesitated. Then stepped aside.

The smell hit first. The chaos. Dogs on every surface. Waste on the floor. Cats huddled in corners.

But they were alive.

And now, they'd get help.

Tommy and his team documented everything. Kai moved through the rooms, calming the animals.

Sienna stayed with the woman, offering resources, explaining the process.

Two hours later, the animals were gone. Safe.

The woman wasn't charged. She was offered services.

Outside, Tommy looked at Kai. "You've got a gift. We could use you—full-time."

"I'll think about it."

Tommy left.

Sienna turned to him. "You should do it. It's sustainable. Legal. Real."

"I know. I'm adjusting."

"You're still making a difference. Just without the mask."

Cole held out a hand. "You did good work today. You'd be a hell of an asset."

Kai shook his hand. "Thanks."

They stood in the parking lot, watching the vans disappear.

"Coffee?" Sienna asked.

Kai nodded. "Yeah. Coffee sounds good."

They walked together toward the café.

Not vigilante and cop.

Just people.

Trying to make things better.

And that, Kai thought, was enough.

Chapter 35
Six Months Later
Kai

Six months later.

Kai stood outside the federal courthouse, watching the crowd gather. Media vans lined the street. Protesters held signs—some supporting Grayson, most condemning him. Cameras were already rolling.

Today was the sentencing.

Kai pulled up his hood and stayed near the back of the crowd. He'd been lying low for months, working quietly, building a new life. But he needed to see this. Needed to know it had all been worth it.

His phone buzzed. A text from Sienna.

You here?

Back of the crowd. You?

Inside. Save you a seat?

I'm good out here. Let me know how it goes.

Will do.

He pocketed the phone and watched the crowd filter inside. At the courthouse entrance, Sienna glanced back and spotted him. She nodded. He nodded in return.

Six months. That's how long it had taken to get here—through federal investigations, grand jury testimony, failed plea deals, and Grayson's endless legal maneuvering.

But the evidence had been overwhelming. Video footage. Breeding logs. Financial records. Testimony from vets, animal control officers, former employees.

The jury had deliberated for less than four hours.

Guilty. On all counts.

And today, Grayson would learn how long he'd spend behind bars.

Kai felt the city around him—the pulse, the signals. Animals still suffering, scattered across the grid. The work was never done.

But it was different now.

He wasn't the Ghost anymore. He was Kai DuMoire. Animal welfare consultant. Working legally—with animal control, with rescue organizations, with detectives like Sienna. Using his gift the right way.

It was slower. Less dramatic. Less cinematic.

But it was real. And it lasted.

The courthouse doors opened. People began spilling out. His phone buzzed again.

Fifteen years. Federal prison. No parole for the first seven. Grayson's done.

Kai stared at the message.

Fifteen years. For a man in his sixties, it was essentially a life sentence.

Justice. Finally.

He typed a reply.

We did it.

We did it. Drinks tonight? Cole's buying.

I'll be there.

He pocketed the phone and walked into the city.

Sienna

Sienna stood on the courthouse steps, watching Grayson being led away in handcuffs. His face was pale. His expensive suit rumpled. His lawyers followed silently, their last motions denied.

Fifteen years. No parole.

It was over.

Cole stepped beside her. "Hell of a sentence."

"He earned it."

"How do you feel?"

"Relieved. Exhausted. Satisfied. All of it."

"You and Kai did good work. You changed things."

"We forced the system to work. That's not quite the same as changing it."

Cole shrugged. "Maybe. But from where I'm standing, you proved it *can* work. When people push. When they refuse to give up."

Sienna smiled faintly. "Maybe."

Mina appeared with a mic in hand, her camera crew close behind.

"Detective Halbrook. Can I get a statement?"

Sienna turned to the camera. "Leonard Grayson has been sentenced to fifteen years in federal prison for animal cruelty, tax evasion, money laundering, and racketeering. Justice has been served. It took too long. The system failed for years. But in the end, the truth came out—and Grayson was held accountable."

"Do you regret anything about how this unfolded?"

"I regret that it took a vigilante and a suspended detective to expose him. I regret that the local system failed. But do I regret stopping him? No. Never."

"What's next for you?"

"The work continues. Animals are still suffering. Cases still need attention. I'm going to keep fighting—with the law, with allies—but also with the understanding that the law isn't always enough."

Mina lowered her mic. "Thank you, Detective. For everything."

"Thank you—for telling the story."

Mina smiled and walked off.

Sienna turned to Cole. "Drinks tonight. My treat."

"Your treat? Must be a special occasion."

"It is. We won."

"We won," Cole echoed.

They descended the courthouse steps, sunlight warming their backs.

Mina

Mina sat in a quiet coffee shop, laptop open, watching the news coverage of Grayson's sentencing. Every major outlet was covering it.

The final chapter.

Her Ghost Rescuer series had won awards. Sparked debate. Changed policy. But the story she cared about most was this one: what happens after justice is served—if it ever is.

She opened a new document.

"After the Ghost: Six Months of Systemic Change"

By Mina Torres

Six months ago, the Ghost Rescuer disappeared. Kai DuMoire stepped out of the shadows and into the light, choosing to work within the system he once defied.

Detective Sienna Halbrook was reinstated after a high-profile review. She returned to duty—with oversight, a new partner, and a deeper understanding of what justice really takes.

And today, Leonard Grayson was sentenced to fifteen years in federal prison.

But the story doesn't end there.

Since Grayson's arrest, the city has changed. Animal control's budget has increased. New protocols have been enacted. A task force has been created to identify illegal breeding operations.

Kai DuMoire now works officially with animal control, using his unique ability to locate animals in distress. In six months, he's helped rescue over forty animals—legally, by the book.

Detective Halbrook now specializes in animal cruelty cases. She's helped build three successful prosecutions since her reinstatement.

The Ghost is gone. But the work continues.

That's the real story. Not the myth. Not the mask. But the quiet, determined work of people who refuse to accept failure. People who believe the system can change.

One case at a time. One animal at a time.

It's not dramatic. But it's lasting.

And it's enough.

Mina smiled and hit publish.

Kai

That evening, Kai met Sienna and Cole at a downtown bar. They grabbed a booth, ordered drinks, and settled into comfortable silence.

"To justice," Cole said, raising his glass. "However messy it is."

"To justice," Sienna echoed.

They clinked glasses.

"So," Cole said, "what now? You two could write books. Do speaking tours."

Sienna laughed. "I'll stick to real detective work."

Cole turned to Kai. "You staying on as a consultant? Or going back to being a locksmith?"

"I'm staying," Kai said. "Tommy offered me a full-time role—salary, benefits, the works."

"You taking it?"

"Yeah. It's good work. And I'm good at it."

Sienna added, "And we work well together. I've got three cases waiting for him."

Kai smiled. "Always more cases."

"Always," Sienna said.

They sipped their drinks.

"Do you miss it?" Cole asked. "The Ghost. The secrecy. The rush?"

"Sometimes," Kai said honestly. "There was something powerful about it. Being more than just me."

"But?"

"But it couldn't last. Eli was right. My dad was right. You burn out. You get caught. You die. And the work stops."

"And now?"

"Now I have support. Allies. A system that's finally starting to work. It's slower. Harder. But it lasts."

Sienna raised her glass again. "To doing it the right way—even when it's harder."

They clinked glasses again.

"How many animals now?" Cole asked.

"Forty-three. Since I went legit."

"Plus sixty from before. Over a hundred lives."

"It's not enough," Kai said quietly. "But it's something."

"It is enough," Sienna said. "You can't save them all. But you can save some. That matters."

Kai nodded. "Yeah. It does."

They paid the tab, stepped out into the night.

The city stretched before them, glittering under the stars.

Animals were still suffering. Still trapped. Still forgotten.

But Kai wasn't alone anymore.

And that made all the difference.

Kai

Later that night, Kai stood alone on the rooftop. The wind brushed his face. The city pulsed below—lights and shadows, noise and silence.

He thought of the dog in the hot car. The first rescue. The mask. The myth. The sixty animals. The sentencing. The work.

It had all led here.

He wasn't the Ghost anymore.

He was Kai DuMoire. A man with an ability. A job. A team.

A man making a difference.

He pulled out his phone. Tommy had sent him a photo: fourteen animals from the hoarding case—healthy, happy, adopted.

Safe.

Kai smiled and slipped the phone away.

The signals were still there. Quieter now. Manageable.

He couldn't save them all.

But he didn't have to.

He turned away from the edge, catching his reflection in a puddle of rainwater.

Not a ghost. Just a man.

And that was enough.

He took the stairs down, stepped into the city.

No more masks. No more shadows. No more myth.

Just the work.

Sienna

The next morning, Sienna sat at her desk, coffee in hand, reviewing files. Six months back on the job. Six months of pushing the system without breaking it.

It had been worth it.

Her phone buzzed. A text from Kai.

Got a signal. Possible breeding op. North side. Industrial district. Want to check it out?

She smiled.

Meet you in thirty. Bringing Cole. Let's do this right. See you there.

She grabbed her jacket. Cole looked up.

"Another case?"

"Another case."

"Lead the way, partner."

They walked out into the morning.

The Ghost was gone.

But the work remained.

And they were ready.

Final Image

The city stirred to life—cars in motion, sunlight slicing through high-rises.

And somewhere in that grid, inside a warehouse on the north side, Kai DuMoire stood beside Detective Halbrook and Detective Reyes, documenting an illegal breeding operation.

No masks. No shadows. No shortcuts.

Just people doing the work. Carefully. Legally. Together.

Kai knelt beside a cage. The dog inside watched him, trembling.

"It's okay," he said softly. "You're safe now."

Behind him, Sienna called in the rescue team. Cole snapped photos. Paperwork was filed.

It wasn't dramatic. It wasn't fast.

But it was justice.

And it was enough.

THE END

Preview: THE SILENT TRADE

Book Two of the DuMoire Series

Kai

The signal hit Kai sometime after two a.m., yanking him from shallow sleep like a hook through flesh.

Not one animal. Not two. Dozens—maybe more. A chorus of terror so intense it made his hands shake.

The signals had been growing stronger for months. His empathic ability expanding, stretching farther into the city. What used to be a whisper was now a scream.

But this—this was different. Not the usual urban suffering: strays, neglect, quiet cruelty. This was acute. Concentrated.

Deliberate.

Terror.

Kai pulled on his jacket, grabbed his tools, and climbed out onto the fire escape. The city sprawled below—Seattle. His new home. His new hiding place. Six months since Grayson. Six months of lying low, working quietly.

But the signals didn't care who he was anymore.

He followed the pull through rain-slicked streets, past shuttered storefronts and dark intersections, toward the waterfront. The docks. Industrial warehouses. The kind of place where things happened that weren't meant to be seen.

The signal intensified near a corrugated metal building—unmarked, unlit, surrounded by chain-link fence. Security cameras. Motion sensors.

A professional operation.

Kai circled until he found a blind spot, scaled the fence, and picked the side door lock in under forty seconds.

Inside, the warehouse was vast. Crates stacked three stories high. Forklifts. Pallets. The air thick with salt, diesel—and fear.

He followed the signal to a row of wooden shipping crates near the loading dock. He crouched by the first one and peered through the slats.

A scarlet macaw stared back at him. Wings clipped. Feathers matted. Eyes dull with shock.

Kai's breath caught.

He moved to the next crate. A spider monkey, barely alive, huddled in the corner.

Next: a ball python, coiled tight, scales dry and cracked.

Exotics. Dozens of them. Trapped. Suffering.

This wasn't a puppy mill.

This was bigger. International.

Kai pulled out his phone and started recording—the crates, the manifests, the shipping labels with foreign ports. Auction house logos. Buyer codes.

Then came voices.

Two men exited a glass-walled office on the far side of the warehouse. One wore a tailored suit. The other, work clothes—nervous, sweating.

"You can't keep doing this," the worker said, voice shaking. "People are asking questions. The inspections—"

"They're handled," said the suited man. Cold. Flat. "You do your job. We do ours."

"But the animals—some are dying in transit. It's not right—"

"It's profitable. That's all that matters."

"I can't be part of this anymore. I'm going to—"

The suited man moved faster than Kai expected. A flash of metal. A suppressed gunshot.

The worker collapsed. Blood spreading across the concrete.

Kai froze. Heart pounding. Breath caught in his throat.

He had just witnessed a murder.

The killer pulled out his phone and made a call. "We have a problem. Send cleanup."

Kai backed away, slow, silent.

Then—*crack.* His foot hit a loose pallet.

The noise echoed.

The suited man's head snapped up. Their eyes locked.

"Hey!"

Kai ran.

Detective Maria Vega

Vega stood in the warehouse just after 4 a.m., staring down at the body. Male. Mid-forties. Port worker ID clipped to his belt. Single gunshot to the chest. Execution-style. No witnesses.

Except—someone *had* been here.

The evidence was clear.

Broken lock on the side door. Fresh scratches. Footprints in the dust leading to the shipping crates.

Someone had seen this.

"Anything?" her partner, Ramos, asked.

"Break-in," Vega said. She knelt, examining the lock. "Clean. Professional. Precise. Whoever did this knew what they were doing."

"Robbery?"

"Nothing missing. Crates are still here. Manifests intact." She rose, walked to a crate, peered through the slats. Empty now—but the smell lingered.

Animals. Exotics.

"What the hell was going on here?"

Her phone buzzed. A text from the captain.

Check your email. Anonymous tip. Might be related.

Vega opened her inbox, found the attachment.

Photos. Dozens of them.

The warehouse. The crates. The animals.

Shipping manifests. Auction house logos. Buyer codes.

And a note.

Some animals are worth killing for. Some people too. This is bigger than one warehouse. Bigger than one city. If you want to stop it, you'll need help. Even from ghosts. —K

She read it twice.

K. Kai DuMoire. The Ghost Rescuer. The vigilante who'd exposed Leonard Grayson and vanished six months ago.

She'd read the case files. Studied the pattern. Clean entries. Lockpick precision. Animal rescues. Halbrook's controversial alliance.

And now he was here. In her city. Tied to a murder.

"Ramos," she said. "We've got a problem."

"What kind of problem?"

"The kind that doesn't stay in the past."

Kai

Kai sat on the roof of his building, watching the sunrise, hands still trembling.

He'd escaped. Barely. The suited man had chased him through the docks, but Kai knew how to vanish.

Still—he'd left a trace. Footprints. Tool marks. Witnessed a murder.

This wasn't like Grayson. This wasn't a corrupt businessman with political ties.

This was something else.

International. Organized. Dangerous.

And Kai couldn't stop it alone.

He pulled out his phone and stared at a contact he hadn't used in six months: *Sienna Halbrook.*

But she was in another city. Another life.

He needed someone *here.* Someone local. Someone who cared more about justice than bureaucracy.

He'd done his research.

Detective Maria Vega. Homicide. Smart. Tenacious. Known for closing impossible cases. Known for bending rules when the rules got in the way.

She was already on the murder. She'd find the signs. She'd connect the dots.

Maybe she'd understand.

Kai attached the photos and typed a message:

Some animals are worth killing for. Some people too. This is bigger than one warehouse. Bigger than one city. If you want to stop it, you'll need help. Even from ghosts. —K

He hit send.

And waited.

Vega

Vega sat in her car outside the warehouse, staring at the message.

Kai DuMoire. The Ghost.

The vigilante who vanished after Grayson fell. Now asking for her help.

She should report him. Forward the message. Put out a BOLO. Treat him like a material witness. Or a suspect.

But she didn't.

Because the photos were real.

The evidence was damning.

And this was bigger than one body on a warehouse floor.

It was the illegal exotic animal trade. A $23 billion black market. Global. Hidden. Protected by money and violence.

And Kai DuMoire was offering to help stop it.

She read the message again. Then typed a reply.

I don't work with vigilantes. But I work cases. If you've got information, meet me. Alone. No tricks. Or I arrest you myself.
—Vega

She hit send.

A moment later, her phone buzzed.

Tomorrow night. Pier 47. Midnight. Come alone. And Detective? Bring an open mind. You're going to need it.

Vega set her phone aside.

The coroner's van pulled away. Crime scene tape flapped in the wind.

She'd spent her whole career following rules. Trusting the system. Believing it could work.

But the system had failed.

Failed the animals.

Failed the whistleblower.

Failed to stop the traffickers.

And now a ghost had come back to finish the job.

Vega didn't know if she could trust him.

Didn't know if she *should*.

She was uncertain about everything—except what she'd do next.

She'd be at Pier 47.
And she was going to find out the truth.
Whatever it cost.

* * *

TO BE CONTINUED IN:

The Silent Trade

Book Two of the DuMoire Series
Some cages are invisible. Some predators wear suits.
Coming Soon

About the Author

L J Ribar is a multi-genre author, cultural researcher, and creative entrepreneur whose passion lies in helping readers and writers find meaning, resilience, and joy through story. With more than 60 books and creative tools published (or in process) under several pen names, Ribar writes across genre, age, and platform to explore what it means to live a fully human life.

His nonfiction titles like **What We Bring to the Party** offer thoughtful guides to culture, creativity, and modern work, while his fiction spans magical archives, road trip survival, haunted hotels, and vigilante rescue missions.

A former software engineer turned full-time creator, Ribar also builds digital tools and writing communities that empower others to share their own stories—like **Writing.Quest**, **CulturesOf.Us**, and many tools for authors in development.

Whether you're here for a vigilante thriller, a soulful journal, a spellbinding adventure, or a clever workbook that helps you focus on what matters, you'll find a warm welcome in this author's catalog.

Visit WineGlassPress.com for more books, resources, and new releases.

Also by L J Ribar

The Atlas of Elsewhere

Some books offer escape. Others offer mirrors. **The Atlas of Elsewhere** offers both—a journey through impossible realms that will lead you back to yourself, transformed

If you've ever wondered about the roads not taken, the choices that shaped you, or the person you might still become, this story is waiting for you.